The God's Daughter

Francis Baffour

Afram Publications (Ghana) Ltd.

Published by:
Afram Publications (Ghana) Limited
P.O. Box M18
Accra, Ghana

Tel: +233 302 412 561, +233 244 314 103
Kumasi: +233 322 047 524/5
E-mail: sales@aframpubghana.com
              publishing@aframpubghana.com
Website: www.aframpubghana.com

First Published, 2015
ISBN: 996470529 8

Acknowledgement

Writing this novel gave me the opportunity to interact with family and friends who gave me thumbs up when the ideas were flowing and I was in a groove and the unfortunate thumbs down when I was not working hard enough. My daughter Fritswa led this group and her encouragement and harassment for me to pick up the manuscript again when it started to collect dust led to the completion of this project. My thanks to Maya Angelou who gave me guidance during the creation of the character, Jackie.

I am grateful for the help and guidance I received from my editor Ohui Allotey, and the Editorial team Afram Publications whose patience and support helped me tremendously in this project.

Finally, I know I could not have completed this book without the support and constructive criticisms of my wife Joan as well as those close relatives who are constantly urging me to become a prolific writer and achieve literary immortality as some of my mentors. I am working on fulfilling their wishes and also on the next manuscript which should be ready soon.

Dedication

Dedicated to the legendary grandmother, Maame Fritswa.
She built a strong, cohesive and loving family.

CHAPTER 1

When the door finally closed behind her, Jackie heaved a great sigh of relief and sank into the brown sofa that had held her mother and aunt during their two-hour conversation. Even though she was in the process of packing for her move, the fact that her mother lived upstairs always made Jackie uneasy. She had a feeling that her mother could come back down for one more chance to convince her to unpack and stay in New York. Nevertheless, in the mind of Mrs. Vance, she had done the best she could to get her daughter and granddaughter to stay and was not about to try anymore.

The soft jazz music from the radio in the kitchen was the only sound Jackie could hear. The occasional street noises from the relatively quiet neighbourhood on Chauncy Street did not even appear to penetrate the cocoon that had enveloped her. Her whole world had shrunk to the living room, and the pressure she had felt from the two women who just left the room still lingered. In spite of the slight doubts, Jackie's mind was made up. In a couple of weeks she will be moving. She was aware of the pain her mother was experiencing because of the love they had for each other, but more especially because of the separation between a grandma and a granddaughter. What else did she have to do, and whom else did she have to convince. Who else was the curse of pain and disappointment going to touch? No one else came to mind. Her brother seemed to understand and appreciate her ambitions so Jackie was not bothered. Unfortunately, the pain touched only those she loved and no one else. Besides, she did not care anymore. A new beginning for her and her daughter was about to be born and that was what mattered to Jackie.

"Thank God," she whispered and closed her eyes as she stretched her heavily drained 145-pound body on the sofa with tears rolling down the corners of her eyes and cascading over her ears.

Jackie Vance had managed to convince everyone who mattered in her family that the main reason for wanting to move to Boston in the summer of 1988 was to advance her career in the insurance industry and to improve on her singing talent. She had secured a position with Prudential Insurance as a manager in the medical claims department, a position similar to the one she now held with an insurance company in New York. She had also made plans to enrol on part time basis at the prestigious Berkeley School of Music to develop her singing talent. After all, that was one reason her mother could not argue with. Mrs. Vance loved her daughter's singing and even though she was going to miss hearing her beautiful voice and music, she understood that it could even be better, so why fault her daughter's desire to enhance her talents.

Jackie and her brother also knew of another reason why she wanted to get out of New York City. A reason she did not share with their mother. And that was because of Charles, her daughter Ama's father. Mrs. Vance could not understand why Jackie would leave home with a ten year old that she was helping to raise and try to raise her by herself as a single parent while working full time and singing part time. Despite the fact that she maintained a similar schedule in New York, her mother was always available to support and take care of Ama. Mrs. Vance felt that her daughter was about to enter the difficult life of single parenthood without the support and care of a loving grandmother for Ama. A life that she experienced when her husband died in a car accident thirty years ago when Jackie was only three. She thought about the pain of raising Jackie and her brother Spike without any help and wondered what life could have been if the rays of life had shone a little brighter in her corner. She was more concerned about Ama whom she adored and felt was more vulnerable than Jackie. The thought of the pain she endured and the tears she shed to raise her two children successfully strengthened her resolve to keep her grandchild home. But much as she tried, Mrs. Vance could not convince her daughter to stay in New York.

At fifteen minutes past ten on that fateful night, she finally gave up on convincing her daughter to stay in New York. The battle to keep Jackie was lost. She kissed her daughter good night, and with tears welling in her eyes was helped by her sister to her upstairs apartment in the two-story brownstone building.

It was past midnight when Jackie finally opened her eyes. Brooklyn has been the home she has ever known and all the good things that had happened in her life had occurred in Brooklyn. She curled her body in the sofa and wrapped her arms around her shoulders to comfort her drained body. The two hours of sleep had not done much to relax her, but she felt the relief of the heavy load that had been lifted off her shoulders with the reluctant understanding of her mother.

"I feel very light," she thought, "and over the next several years I know I will be carrying a load I have never experienced. I can't fail Ama, I can't fail myself and I can't fail Mom. There is too much at stake here and I just can't afford to slip. Merciful Father guide me", she prayed. "Strengthen me and give me the wisdom to chart my course through the traps and trials that lay ahead of me. I have to move on, I have to move on," she continued with a determined expression on her face and the habitual tightened lips when she was fighting the odds or being stubborn.

Several ideas and thoughts raced through her head at varying speeds as she lay on the sofa imagining what life would bring in the days and years ahead. With the help of her best friend Brenda Morris, who had moved to Boston from New York several years ago, Jackie knew her life would still be good and she could take good care of her daughter although she knew that she could not do better than her mother.

Brenda was like the sister Jackie never had. She has been Jackie's best friend since they were both seven years old. They both went to Stuyvesant High School on 16th Street and 1st Avenue in Manhattan before Brenda left the city to go to Boston College. Even though Jackie visited her friend on several occasions in Boston College, she never thought that there would come a time when she would consider living in Boston. Her childhood impressions about Boston being the most racist city in the Northeast were deeply implanted and Brenda was never able to convince her friend that racism in Beantown was no different than Brooklyn, Providence or for that matter any other city in the United States. Brenda was the godmother of Ama whom she nicknamed Pumpkin and she always dreamed of having her closer.

Jackie's relationship with Charles, Ama's father, a lawyer by training but working as a high-flying investment banker with Merrill Lynch, suited her well. To Jackie, the emotional stress during her pregnancy when during a heated argument with Charles, he questioned her faithfulness and the possibility that she may have slept with someone else, was unforgivable. One could understand the jealousies of an insecure man who could not stand other men admiring or trying to date his beautiful girlfriend, but, Jackie could not understand nor forgive Charles for questioning her faithfulness and trust after she became pregnant.

Jackie Vance was considered to be the most attractive woman on the campus of Columbia University and she attracted the attention of most men, black and white. She was aware of her beauty and enjoyed the attention she commanded. However, as Charles' girlfriend during their college days, she stayed faithful and never cheated on him no matter what disagreements or fights they had. Charles could not make a similar claim if she asked him, but she couldn't be bothered. She was madly in love and the whole world knew that.

Jackie was stubborn and independent-minded just like her brother Spike. So when she made up her mind to ignore Charles and get on with her life, there was no turning back. Besides, she was set on developing her career and no one was going to interfere with her dreams. She was not ready for marriage and was capable of taking care of herself and her child. Obviously she was aware that her mother was always available to help take care of Ama in times of crisis and that also influenced her thinking and decisions. In her mind, she could get married whenever she was ready and there would be a line of men stretching as far as the eye can see beating a path to date her.

Jackie always treated Charles with respect ever since they met on the campus of Columbia University and started dating when she was a sophomore. Her respect for Charles did not dissolve with the problems that ensued when she became pregnant. However, she made a commitment to herself to raise Ama without him. Except for the times when Charles felt like playing the role of a father, the flexibility of the situation also suited him well because he was not ready for marriage either. The huge salary and the pressures of Wall Street kept him busy, and he sometimes stupidly used it as an excuse for not making time to see his daughter.

Jackie was almost always intoxicated with work and very few could keep up with her intensity and pace of work. Very energetic and detail oriented, she managed to clear up a two-month backlog of unprocessed claims in her department within three weeks of joining New York Mutual. Obviously her prior high profile experience in operations management and her participation in the development of sophisticated operational systems for claims processing in her prior job facilitated her work at New York Mutual. Even though she considered her weekend singing in a jazz nightclub as a hobby, her boss considered it the extra work that really showed the extent of her stamina and talent.

A week before she was to move to Boston, Jackie was thrown into a situation she had not dreamed about or imagined could happen. She had received an offer from another insurance company based in Baltimore for an executive position. Through a contact from Charles and earlier interviews for a position at USF&G it seemed that the Baltimore opportunity would materialise. But, the whole process stalled and Jackie put it out of her mind. However, for some strange reason, the vice president position she had forgotten about resurfaced and the insurance company made her an offer with an attractive salary. Jackie was offered a twenty percent salary increase, but it had come with the stress of making another decision that meant turning down the offer from Boston immediately and changing her plans, mindset and dreams from Boston to Baltimore. She was not sure about how she could continue singing in Baltimore because she did not know the city well and did not have the support she knew she and Ama would get from Brenda in Boston. The professional opportunity was incredible, the money was better than she had ever dreamed about and Charles and Spike had strongly articulated all the positive aspects of the new job and why she should accept the offer. Jackie was clearly torn between what she knew life would be in Boston and the unknown in Baltimore. Deep down she knew what the better option was, and after a short consultation with her mother she made a decision.

Spike was still friendly with Charles but never really cared for him. He only wanted him to be a responsible father to his niece and respect his sister. He kept in touch with Charles once in a while and met him for basketball games.

Thinking back to how it all started, Jackie knew that Charles still had strong feelings for her but she was not ready to invest the energy and time to renew the relationship. She was comfortable with her life and had all the support systems she needed. The contacts between her and Charles had also been infrequent so Jackie could not imagine that she would ever get such help from Charles to secure the USF&G position. But then, she rationalised that they were still good friends and parents, and Charles' help could be his way of also helping his own daughter. If there was another reason for his help, Charles had not made it clear to her and she was not eager to find out. She thought about her new $186,000 annual salary job plus bonuses and other fringe benefits and tightened her lips before breaking into a smile as she hugged her daughter very tightly.

"Maa, Maa, why are you hugging me too tight?"

Jackie did not answer.

"Maa, Maa, you are squeezing the air out of me."

She still did not answer.

"Maa, I am losing all the air in me."

The little girl sensed that something might not be right or very right. She felt her mother wiping her face and realised that she could be crying. As she released the child from the tight hug, Ama confirmed her suspicion when she saw tears rolling down her mother's face.

"What is it, Maa?"

"Oh, my baby," she said as Ama sat next to her.

Jackie looked into those spotless black and white eyes of her daughter and responded, "I am very happy and just feeling good". She paused for a moment, tightened her lips again and thought about what lay ahead, especially for the child and said, "My Angel, we are moving to Maryland to begin a new life".

Ama was confused about her mother being so happy and crying with those tight lips. She sadly asked, "Why?"

"Because it is a good opportunity for us. Yes. Yes. Yes. We are on our way, and I am going to make life wonderful for you, baby."

"Really?"

"Yes, really my dear. We are going to buy a beautiful house and do all the wonderful things you always want to do."

"A new house?"

"Yes a new house and anything you want in your room."

"But I thought we were going to Boston to stay with Ms. Brenda."

"You will love our new life." Jackie ignored the question.

"Really Maa?" she asked with a tinge of disbelief.

"Yes, my dear, yes, yes, yes. Let's get ready to step out for a moment."

"We are going out?"

"Yes Pumpkin let's go".

"Where?"

"I want to send a special thank you to your father."

"So where are we going?"

"Into the city."

Jackie did some shopping at Bloomingdales and at about 6 o'clock Spike met them as she had requested, in front of the department store. Together, they ordered flowers to be delivered to Charles with a simple note that said, "Thank you, Charles. We are Baltimore Bound, Love Ama and Jackie."

"I am hungry," said Jackie.

"I am hungry too," echoed Ama.

"I have a great idea. Why don't we go to our favourite seafood restaurant and celebrate?"

"That's exactly what I want. Some seafood," Jackie agreed.

"Let's go to Legal Seafood."

"That sounds like a great idea. I have been there before. Remember Ma, remember?"

"Yes I do".

CHAPTER 2

*T*he doorbell rang twice while she was in the middle of a bestselling novel on South Africa. It was a thriller that had consumed the better part of the day and kept her rooted to a recliner for a couple of hours. She wasn't ready yet to put the book down but she remembered that this adorable new neighbour was coming to visit so she reluctantly proceeded to rise from her chair. Before she could mark the page and put the book away, the doorbell rang again. Mae Brown quickly dropped the book next to her black reclining chair while thinking, "Goodness, this little girl must be impatient." She dragged her six-foot frame off the chair, removed her reading glasses, stretched her limbs and headed for the door.

"I will be right there, young girl," her voice boomed across the room.

"All right," said Ama as Mae approached the door.

"How are you, my dear?" she said trying to soften the deep voice that has defined her personality and helped her win several speaking engagements and commentaries on television and as a narrator in documentary films.

"I am fine," replied Ama as she walked past Mae into foyer leading to the living room.

"What did you say is your name again?" Mae asked to start the conversation.

"My name is Ama."

"Ama? What a beautiful name. I also have a friend called Ama."

"Is she also from Ghana?"

"Yes she is from Ghana."

"Is she my age?"

"No not at all. She's a very nice woman. Actually, we went to school together in Boston several years ago, but she is back in Ghana now. She is a nun."

"A nun? That's cool."

"Why? Do you know any nuns?"

"Yes. There were nuns in my kindergarten school," she said nodding her head to stress her point. "Is your friend called Sister Ama?"

"No. Actually she is Sister Magdalene but I still call her Ama because we are very close friends. I realise that you know my name, because you called me this morning when I was driving in. Right?"

"Yes Miss Brown. My mother watches you on television all the time. I think she also showed me three books that you wrote."

"Really."

"Yes. Do you write a lot?"

"Sometimes. So you've seen some of my TV programs."

"Yes."

"And you know about me?"

"Yea" she said, blowing a pink bubble gum that exploded to engulf her perfect nose and chin with a loud pop.

"I am glad to hear that, Ama. I wish many children will continue to watch the programs on Africa. Unfortunately, I will not be doing the 'Back to the Roots' program anymore."

"Why?" She asked unemotionally as she tore the gum

from her chin.

"Well."

"My mother will be disappointed to hear that, because she watches your programs and always wants me to learn more about Africa. Actually, I don't think she knows much about Africa."

"What makes you think so?"

"Just from what she says."

"That may not necessarily be correct."

"Yeah, that's true."

"What a grown lady in a ten year old body," Mae thought and smiled to herself, exposing her perfect set of white teeth.

"Don't worry; I am sure they will find someone to continue the program. Besides, I am now your neighbour so you can always come and see some of my photographs and slides from Africa and other parts of the world."

"Really?"

"Yes, really."

"Thanks, Miss Brown. Thanks."

"You're welcome."

"Can my mother come too?"

"Of course. And you can bring some of your friends too."

"But, I don't have any here."

"Well, not yet."

"I know."

"You will meet one very soon," Mae said thinking about her niece.

Mae and her little friend walked into the kitchen like old friends, and before Mae could offer her something to drink, Ama had already fired three questions in rapid succession about the African sculpture pieces in the living room.

Mae Brown's living room looked more like the Museum of African Art than the living room of a middle-aged successful writer, poet, businesswoman and professor of African-American studies. The living room was huge and exquisitely decorated and lighted. On one section of the wall was a collection of West African sculptural pieces including priceless carvings from Nigeria, Benin and Ghana. On the opposite wall were pieces from Zaire, the Congo and East Africa. There are also two beautiful Mende masks from Sierra Leone believed to be over a thousand years old given to her in 1974 by the then President of Sierra Leone whom she claims fell in love with her. The masks were uniquely outstanding and it depicted beauty and elegance in womanhood. Her collection also included very old figurines depicting Dogon art history from ancient Mali and assorted dolls. All the beautiful sculpture and art pieces were held together by an expensive Persian rug given to her by the Shah of Iran during a visit to Teheran in 1977.

Mae thrived on her reputation as a collector of priceless African art and enjoyed the recognition and respect she enjoyed from her colleagues and adversaries. Modesty was not one of her strongest virtues especially when her white colleagues came to visit and she had the opportunity to show off her collection and talk about her travels. Once, when she was stepping over the bounds of exaggeration for the fifteenth time at a party in her honour where she also had the opportunity to show off her collection, her sister whispered, "Let's be modest here, Mae. You are beginning to sound ridiculous."

But Mae was quick to whisper back, "Modesty my butt. I'm selling sis, I'm selling. They don't know a thing about what I'm talking about."

"I hope they buy."

"They've bought a lot already, girrrl."

"Thanks."

"You bet."

Mae never disclosed the real sources of her collections, especially those she considered priceless pieces except for the countries from which she obtained them. Her thinking was that disclosing everything about her pieces might diminish the significance and value of her collection. That was the sort of reasoning her sister always had problems with. But she was not persuasive enough to convince Mae to change her thinking or reasoning.

The lighting in the living room was perfectly done and the figurines and other smaller pieces housed in a glass case in the family room enhanced the elegance of the room. In fact, it was believed that she had given many of her collections to a museum in New York and the Smithsonian for safekeeping and exhibitions.

"I will tell you more about the pieces later".

"Okay."

"What an inquisitive mind," Mae thought.

"I will be very glad when all this moving is over so I can show you our house," said Ama with a look of frustration.

"I know what you mean. Moving is unpleasant and very tiring. I am sure your mother and uncles must be tired. Have you been helping them?"

"Not really. But only one of them is my uncle," she was quick to correct Mae. "He tells me that I get in their way all the time and he screams and blames me when he can't get things done right."

"Is that right?"

"I try to stay away until they ask me to do something."

"He screams at you and blames you?"

"Yes."

"That's not nice."

"That's Uncle Spike, all right."

"Oh boy," Mae marvelled at her quickness.

"I know that Mom will ask me to clean my room as soon as they finish unpacking." She sipped a mouthful of the chilled apple juice Mae had poured her and sank into a black leather sofa. She looked very adorable in her flowered jumpsuit and sneakers with her hair flowing down both sides of her head in two long corn rolls.

Mae poured a glass of seltzer water and settled in the chair opposite her and the television set so she could get a good look at her pretty round face and prominent eyes.

"Okay, now tell me about yourself since you are the new girl on the block".

"Okay", she said with an expression that seemed to say I am ready for you, what do you want to know?

"How old are you?"

"I just turned eleven, but my Uncle always tells me I am going on twenty."

"Twenty?"

"He always says that I am too smart for my age."

"I am sure he's right." Mae realised right away that she was about to engage a conversation with a mature eleven year old. In fact, she had concluded that Ama's uncle was indeed right that the little girl was approaching twenty. "You are indeed a smart girl."

"Not that smart, Miss Brown."

"Well I think you are."

"May be I am," she said with a serious face while Mae

stared.

Mae Brown smiled to herself as she thought that Ama would be a very interesting girl to have around as a neighbour. She definitely would make up for the little girl Mae never had.

"Hopefully her mother will not mind sharing this angel with me. I love her already," Mae thought.

As she walked back to the kitchen to refill her glass, Mae looked through the window and saw the gentleman she thought to be Ama's uncle. He had just taken what appeared to be the last box from the U-Haul truck and closed the door.

"What's your Uncle's name again?'

"Uncle Spike."

"Spike?"

"Yes, my uncle is called Spike. Spike Vance. He is my Mom's older brother."

Spike was a hard core New Yorker who could not envision living anywhere else but in Brooklyn. Even though he was a successful producer with ABC News and had travelled extensively both in the U.S. and overseas, he was still married to his neighbourhood like a typical Brooklyn boy. At five feet five inches, he was too small for the tough guy reputation and the sharp tongue he had developed in the neighbourhood. Spike was synonymous with New York Knicks. He almost always wore New York Knicks caps and in fact, believed when he was in high school that he would start as a point guard for the Knicks during his lifetime. Obviously, at thirty-five, the Knicks dream had not materialised. Nevertheless, he was always a fixture at the home games of the Knicks. The only difference between him and other well-known diehard Knicks fans was that the television cameras did not focus on him as a nationally known celebrity. However, he was well known in his neighbourhood in Brooklyn.

Spike was also well-respected because of the reputation he cultivated as a good basketball player on the McLaughlin playgrounds off Flatbush Avenue and Tillary Street. With the help of his own self-promotion, he became known as "the Banker". Whenever the outcome of a basketball game was on the line and his team was a basket away from winning, he would usually scream, "give me the rock give me the rock," and the ball in his hands was equivalent to having money in the bank because it was a guaranteed two points. He would either make the shot or create a foul by a self-initiated contact and be the first to scream, "Foul, foul, you fouled me." As good as Spike was on the neighbourhood playgrounds, he did not make it through college on basketball scholarship. He made it through NYU with the help of his mother and through his own hard work. He was an exceptionally bright student who went through college with academic scholarships and graduated Summa cum Laude. Considered a role model in his neighbourhood, Spike hardly missed block parties or the Saturday basketball pick-up games whenever he was off from work. He also adored his sister and considered her to be his best friend.

Mae began to wonder who could be the child's father, but then realised that Ama had not talked about her father being one of the men unloading the truck so she didn't pursue the subject. Instead she proceeded to ask her about their trip from Boston.

It was a long trip to the suburbs of Baltimore taking almost eight hours. Mae did not expect the next door neighbours to come visiting. She felt that it was a bit too soon for her to also go over to say hello. After all, she had established a warm friendship with their emissary, Ama, and unlike the family that used to live in that house she had positive feelings about being friends with Jackie and her family.

"Did uncle Spike drive the truck from Boston?"

"Yes, but I think his friend Peter helped him. I drove with Mom in our car behind them. I know that the very tall man with large ears who is helping us does not drive."

"Large ears? And how do you know that he doesn't drive?"

"My Mom says he doesn't have a license. I think he is Uncle Spike's girlfriend's brother. Uncle Spike always makes fun of his ears."

"That's not nice of Uncle Spike."

"Yes, and my mother always tells him that."

"Your mother must be lucky to have all these strong men helping her. Hopefully, they will finish unpacking soon."

"I hope they do."

"So you can fix up your room?"

"Not really."

Mae smiled again at her quick answers and asked, "Isn't it quite warm today?", as refilled the child's glass.

*   *   *

Even though Jackie said hello and waved to Mae with the warmest smile she had seen in weeks, the beauty of the little girl who called her name caught Mae's attention. The hellos were brief except that of Ama who like any talkative eleven year old was not brief. In fact, she went closer to Mae and tried to engage her in a conversation. The excitement of meeting a TV personality was evident in the little girl's actions. To make the child who had just captured her imagination happy, Mae invited her to stop over later on in the evening.

Thinking about their brief encounter earlier on during the day with her new neighbours, it occurred to Mae that she did not even know the name of the little girl's mother.

"What's your mother's name, Ama?"

"Her name is Jackie, but some of her friends call her Lady Day."

"Lady Day? That's an interesting name, but why?"

"Well, I think because she sings very well like Billy Holiday that's why her friends call her that."

"Are you sure?"

"Yes. She sings very well. She even sang in jazz clubs in Boston".

"She must be a very talented woman. Can you sing too?"

"No I can't sing. In fact, my Mum tells me that I have to join the children's choir in my church to learn how to sing".

Mae Brown and Ama spent about thirty minutes chatting about everything from life in Boston, her school, the Catholic sisters in her kindergarten school to what life would be like in Baltimore. Before she left, Mae asked her to stop by again to visit.

Long after Ama had left, Mae had dinner with her sister Daisy Rae as usual. She told Daisy Rae about her new neighbours, Jackie Vance and her daughter Ama and what a lovely little girl she was. The sweetness of the little girl and the angelic look in her eyes reminded Mae how beautiful innocence was. It reminded her of her friend, Sister Magdalene and her innocence and naivety. It reminded her of the wonderful conversations she had with Sister Magdalene when they shared an apartment on Massachusetts Avenue in Cambridge during their student days in Harvard. She remembered the trust, closeness and friendship of Sister Magdalene and how the nun helped her through some of the most difficult times in Harvard, especially when her mother died. The nun's prayers and warmth convinced Mae that there was indeed a living God somewhere out there who listened and responded positively to those who asked for his help. In Ama's innocence, Mae remembered the strengths and the special qualities of her friend.

However, on the beautiful face of the little girl, Mae also saw vulnerability. The qualities that seemed to remind her of her own innocence at a time when she thought she should have known more about life than her roommate who possibly had lived a more sheltered life in a convent. Mae tried hard not to remember those chilly, wintry and lonely nights in Cambridge when her mother died, but try as she did, she couldn't push all the nightmares away.

It was then that she realised that her fears and disappointments were deeply rooted than she always thought. In fact, she was convinced after her trip to Ghana in the spring of 1972 that she had finally come to accept the finality of her mother's death. But, after all those years, the pretty little girl had reminded her that she still needed the likes of Sister Magdalene as friends.

On the fifth day after their arrival, Mae finally decided that it was time to invite Jackie and her family over for dinner. She had met them again on the second day of their arrival in front of their house and exchanged the courteous neighbourly welcomes. She met Uncle Spike, his friend Peter and the tall man called Eddie, whom Ama referred to as "Uncle Spike's girlfriend's brother".

"A bunch of nice people", she thought. Jackie looked prettier than Mae thought when she first saw her. She reasoned that the lady was very tired after the long trip from Boston and couldn't have looked or felt any better.

It exactly 7.30 in the evening, the doorbell rang. Luckily, dinner was almost ready and Mae's sister Daisy Rae had finished setting the table. Mae answered the door, and in came Jackie, Ama and Spike. The other gentlemen had gone back to New York a couple of days earlier.

"How are you Ama?"

"I am quite well, thank you," she responded.

"Hello Ms. Brown," Jackie said with Spike echoing the greeting.

"Hello Jackie, Hello Spike. Come on in, come in my dear," said Mae in her usual deep voice.

"By the way, meet my sister Daisy Rae and her daughter Bianca."

"Hello Daisy Rae," said Jackie as she shook her hand and patted the nine year-old Bianca on the shoulder and hugged her.

Spike also shook Daisy Rae's hand and added, "I love the name Daisy Rae. I have a friend Daisy Rae Stallings and you certainly remind me of her."

Jackie chatted briefly with Bianca and complimented her on her beautiful braids. Ama gravitated to Bianca, shook hands with her and quickly vanished into the family room with her before she could say hello to Daisy.

"Come back here Ama and say hello to Bianca's mother," said Jackie.

"Leave 'em alone. Let them go and have fun," interrupted Daisy Rae, but Ama came back with Bianca in tow to say hello and quickly vanished again.

Unlike Mae, Daisy Rae was very slim but they were both tall women and elegant. She had a very short well-groomed haircut, a style for which she has been identified for over ten years. She was also light skin coloured unlike her sister. But like her sister, Daisy Rae is also an educator. She was an elementary school teacher-trainer and coordinator in the Baltimore School System. She had a reputation as a strong disciplinarian, a trait she learned from their father, a Baptist minister from the Carolinas.

The Vances and Mae waited in the cosy family room and chatted about life in Baltimore as Daisy Rae put finishing touches to the meal Mae had helped to prepare. Daisy Rae loved to cook and was the type of woman who could stay up for hours to cook for an entire army. She always reminded Mae of their mother when they had to prepare big meals during their family reunions in North Carolina. But as good as Daisy Rae was, she lacked that special touch of their mother. That special touch which Mae always believed came with years of cooking experience. In fact, Mae was convinced that their mother was a gifted cook just as others were gifted painters.

Dinner was roasted chicken, spare ribs, stir fried vegetables in soy sauce, corn bread, rice and French fries. Jackie was more fascinated with the decorations and paintings in the house than the good food Daisy Rae had prepared. The dining room was rather simply decorated with colonial furniture on an Indian rug with some African and Haitian paintings decorating the wall. Mae did not do much talking during dinner. Jackie actually became the centre of attraction as Mae asked her to tell them about her singing. She told them about how she started in the children's choir of the Mariners Baptist Temple church in the Chinatown of New

York before joining the famous Brooklyn Tabernacle Singers. Jackie got them all laughing when she talked about hating piano lessons when her mother forced her to play the piano. She complained about the teacher, the music sheets, the piano and anything in her vicinity as irritants that prevented her from concentrating. Jackie just hated the discipline of practicing the piano. She was very talented and could easily have become an excellent piano player like her brother rather than a singer. She gave credit to Spike for encouraging her to start singing jazz songs. Jackie did not make a big deal about her singing talent because she did not feel she was that good. She however, made a deal with Mae to sing them a song after dinner if she was spared the ordeal of telling the story of how she embarrassed herself during her first nightclub act in Brooklyn.

When they retired to the family room after dinner and waited for dessert, Mae set up her slide projector as Jackie sang the jazz tune "God bless the child" with a piano accompaniment by her brother. The room burst into a loud applause when she finished, with the children and Spike pumping their arms in the air and shouting, "Whouu, whouu, whouu......."

"Girrrl you can sing," exclaimed Mae.

"I am really impressed," said Daisy Rae.

"Thank you."

"You certainly have a great voice, girrrl. You are really good," said Mae with deep admiration.

"Thank you."

"Maybe we could get you to sing in our choir," said Daisy Rae.

"Welllllll, maybe."

"Why, maybe?"

"I'm just not ready yet."

"Since you don't belong to any church here at the moment, at least you could join our church to start with."

"Okay, I will think about that, but I don't know if I can join a choir yet."

"Maa you can," Ama interrupted.

"Listen to her. You should be joining the choir," said Spike holding Ama in his arms.

"That was really good, Jackie," Mae said again and added, "let's have dessert as we see these slides of my trip to Rome three weeks ago. I haven't had time to see the slides myself."

"Rome? That's cool," said Ama.

"Did you see the Pope?" Bianca asked.

"Yes, I did."

"You did?"

"Yes, my dear."

"How was he?"

"He looked very well to me."

"Did he bless you?" asked Ama.

"Yes, he did."

"Wow, that's cool."

Desert was pecan pie and vanilla ice cream.

"Mae you just discovered one of my weaknesses," Jackie confessed.

"What's that?" asked Bianca.

"She can't resist pecan pie," answered Spike.

"You and me, both," said Daisy Rae.

"Well, enjoy it," Mae said.

"Just ignore me if I go for seconds."

Mae told them about her trip to Rome to meet her friend and former roommate, Sister Magdalene and the Archbishop of Kumasi, the Rev. Frederick Kwasi Kwarpong. She showed off pictures of her meeting with the Pope before the slide show began. Mae also took the opportunity to announce her invitation by the bishop to go to Ghana and teach at the University of Cape Coast for a year.

Mae had always entertained the idea of teaching in Ghana for a while since her first visit to the country several years ago, but she has been busy with her own teaching schedule at Johns Hopkins University, writings, television productions and several speaking engagements. As a result, the idea of taking a sabbatical and teaching in Ghana had not been in the forefront of her plans until she met Sister Magdalene and the bishop in Rome. Evidently, they were able to convince Mae.

Having decided that she would eventually go to Ghana in December, and was thinking and dreaming about the country she would be living in for about ten months, she decided to show some slides of her previous visits to Ghana and other African states. Mae showed about one hundred slides of several interesting places. She showed various castles and the forts that were built in the fifteenth and sixteenth centuries. She told the history of some of the buildings and their significance as bases for the slave trading and commerce for the Europeans. During the slide show, she compared the culture in West Africa to that of Black America and wondered about the similarities that some people have often claimed existed.

"There is the perception that a majority of the present day African Americans in the new world represent African culture. I find that very wrong, wrong and wrong."

"Why do you say that?" asked Jackie.

"Simply because there is no comparison here to what is over there. You have to live in that culture to appreciate what

I am talking about," replied Mae.

"How come?" Spike wondered.

"The representation of the African culture in black America is not in its purest form. In fact, it's not even close. There have been much Westernisation and adulteration of the various cultures since the end of slavery, and that is understandable to some extent," said Daisy Rae.

"I can understand that," Spike said.

"Actually, the real African culture is completely missing."

"Oh yes," Jackie concurred with Mae, "that's understandable."

"Yes, I don't see how else things could be any purer here than what it is over there, because there is so much American or western influence in our lives," said Spike. "Besides, this is America and not Africa."

"That's exactly right," interjected Mae, and continued, "that's why we must seriously re-establish our link with our roots."

"I agree," said Spike.

"Especially if we call ourselves African-Americans."

"Does that mean we are going to live in Africa?" asked Ama.

"Yes, maybe some of us have to, my dear," answered Jackie.

Mae decided to take over the conversation and tell them a little bit about the nature of the people she has dealt with for a long time and specifically about Ghanaians among whom she will be living in the next few months.

"The African culture, as diverse and complex as the number of different groups there are, is totally unique. The discipline and the unique way they live have been woven into the fabric of the daily lives of the people. It is amazing. Indeed it is amazingly powerful and pure. Take the Fantes and Asantes for example. I happen to know a bit about those two groups and their cultures. They are a group of proud people whose intelligence and activities rivalled the so-called ancient civilisations. The Asante Empire, for instance was once the most powerful empire in West Africa and it stretched way beyond the present borders of Ghana. Its army were extremely powerful, disciplined and the most feared by the British when they tried to invade the inland territories of the then Gold Coast. The Asante army defeated the British in many wars. Their intelligence gathering, use of advance scouts to assess enemy troop strengths and tactical manoeuvres, especially between the seventeen hundreds and 1852 when some of the fiercest wars between them and other armies were fought, really showed the power of those people. Those same traits are still evident in the unadulterated Asante, and I mean those who are not influenced by the western society."

"You are not talking about an Asante in the Bronx?" Spike joked.

"No Spike."

"I know a few Asantes in the Bronx."

"Even some of the Asantes and Fantes in New York try to maintain certain aspects of their culture and I have experienced some of it," Mae stressed.

"The power and strength of those people can best be described by the blood, sweat, tears and horrors of abuse they endured as slaves and the journeys they made across the seas in tightly packed ships for several weeks. I can tell you more about the culture and lives of Ghanaians because I have associated with them, studied them and lived in the country. And you can only appreciate what I am talking about if you actually live with them," said Mae.

"Well I hope you are not talking about the westernised Ghanaians," Daisy Rae interrupted.

"Even the so-called westernised Ghanaians were brought up with the same values and honour, and live their lives in the same cultural values. Believe me it's amazing as is different."

"This sounds interesting," said Jackie.

"Oh believe me, it is. You'll live a good life in the major cities and think that those there have forgotten about their culture, but you should see them in their homes. It's even more pronounced during some of their festivals or ceremonies. You will appreciate the depth of these people," said Daisy Rae who had visited Ghana once.

"Daisy, you don't even have to go beyond Accra to see rich culture. Have you forgotten about the Gas and their traditions. Certainly you haven't forgotten about that Ga festival and the funeral you talked so much about," interrupted Mae.

"Oh, yes."

"Jackie, that funeral ceremony in Kumasi for a prominent businessman who was also from the royal family, blew my mind."

"It's an experience I will encourage every African-American to live. We have to live it, feel it and touch it to appreciate what we have as a people."

"Maybe we can visit Ghana while you are there," said Jackie and added, "it will especially be good for these children."

"Yeah Mom."

"Yes, yes, yes, it will be real good," echoed Bianca.

"You bet it will be. These kids know nothing about real culture except for TV, rap music and Nickelodeon," said Spike as he tickled his niece.

"No that's not true," protested Bianca.

"What do you know about African culture?" asked her

mother.

"I'm not telling."

"Jackie, it will be a wonderful experience for these children if you could make it to Ghana while I am there. You will certainly have the benefit of my presence there and wouldn't have to worry about accommodation and a tour guide."

"Thanks, I may do that."

"Would you girls like to visit Africa?" asked Mae.

"Yes," they responded in unison.

"But do they speak English?" asked Ama.

"This is exactly what I am talking about," replied Mae. "Yes, most of them speak English and in addition, they speak other languages which we don't, my dear."

"Like what?" asked Bianca.

"Well there are hundreds of languages spoken in Africa and I can't even begin to name them all because I don't know but a few."

"I am sure you can learn a few words and a whole lot more about the African and the continent when you visit," said Daisy Rae.

Mae concluded the slide show with a story about her visit to the Cape Coast Castle and how she broke down and cried when she was shown the dungeons in which the slaves were held, and how they were treated before being transported to the Americas. The stories Mae told about the castles and slavery peaked Jackie's interest to visit West Africa and to take advantage of Mae's invitation to Ghana.

"There is the grand castle of 'em all in Elmina."

"Elmina?" asked Spike.

"Yes. Elmina is a fishing town about six miles from where I will be teaching at the University of Cape Coast. I was not able to visit that castle but it's the biggest in West Africa and the oldest."

"How old?" asked Jackie.

"Over five hundred years old. It was built by the Portuguese in 1482."

"Goodness, I can't wait to see that."

"Come to think of it, that town is far older than our country," said Spike.

"Well, to really indicate how old it is, think about this.

Columbus went to that town long before he set out on his journey to discover the Americas," Mae said to the surprise of the children.

"Believe me Ms. Brown, if it's all right with you, we will accept your invitation and come over sometime next year when it is convenient," said Jackie.

"I'll be delighted to see you there, and I hope you can make it to Ghana."

"We'll be there."

CHAPTER 3

*L*ife on the campus of the University of Cape Coast was a relaxing and a refreshing change for Mae. The campus was less than a quarter of a mile from the Atlantic Ocean and the perpetual smell of the sea in the air was most refreshing especially in the mornings. From the balcony of her three-bedroom home, Mae had a splendid and majestic view of the Atlantic Ocean. Waking up in the morning to see the sun emerge from the east through the coconut trees that lined the entire coast for miles was the most beautiful scene she claimed to have ever seen. Mae was fascinated with the huge waves that constantly crashed the shores with tremendous force and often wondered how the beaches have withstood such pounding for years and still remained pristine and not eroded. Whenever she could on weekends, and on certain evenings, she would go to the beach to read or just watch the fishermen bring in their catch. She enjoyed the beautiful melodic songs the fishermen sang and the assorted percussion instruments they played as they pulled in fish with dragnets to the rhythmic songs. She sometimes engaged the fishermen in long conversations and made friends with many of them. She learned about the various fishing techniques used by the men and heard several fishing stories. Quite often she went home with lots of fresh fish from her fishing friends.

To the west of Cape Coast was Elmina, the ancient and famous town that had always fascinated and intrigued Mae. She deliberately refused to visit the castle until Jackie and the children arrived in Ghana. She went to Elmina on a few occasions to enjoy music at the newly built Elmina Beach Hotel and socialise with friends. On one weekend she went there with her friend Bishop Kwarpong to celebrate the 80th birthday of one of the Bishop's best friends. Called RP by most of his friends and in fact, the entire country, the man was in the Bishop's opinion, the most brilliant and smartest man he had ever known. RP was once the vice chancellor of the Kwame Nkrumah University of Science and Technology in Kumasi, a city where the bishop was born and has lived for most of his life.

Entering the family house of RP in the heart of Elmina township, the bishop shouted the name of his friend from the bottom of the steps leading to the balcony of the first floor. He led Mae up the stairs to RP who was waiting in a wheel chair and beaming with a big smile. The bishop held his hand, spoke in his ears for a brief moment and they both burst out in laughter.

"That must be a good joke," said Mae as she shook the hand of this great man the bishop had talked so much about.

"Yes, it's one of our old jokes," said the bishop and then introduced Mae to his friend saying "Mae, this is the man that I have been telling you so much about. He just exudes power, brilliance and immense knowledge from his pores."

"I have heard so much about you."

"I hope they kept the bad stuff to themselves."

"He's such a modest man."

"I have no doubts," Mae said.

"He's blessed."

"Thanks for the compliments, but please remember that your friend has a tendency to exaggerate," said RP.

"I admire your humility, Bob."

"Just cut it out," RP replied.

"Are you embarrassed?"

"You know better than that."

"I thought so."

"That's right."

"Mae, I told you that he is also very humble."

"Thanks for the compliments," responded RP with a chuckle.

Joined by RP's sister, the four sat on the balcony overlooking a park filled with playing children and other inhabitants going about their business and enjoyed the evening while listening to RP talk about the history, symbolisms and parties involved in the Bakatue festival. This is a festival that Mae has been dying to enjoy and was waiting to experience with her guests from America.

"Frankly I think the best thing for you to do is to try and attend as many of the events of the festival and I hope you will find the time to do that. I don't expect you to be able to do that, because of your schedule and when some of these activities take place. But, if there is anything I can do to facilitate your stay in this area, please let me know and I will gladly do it," RP offered.

"Thank you very much. This seems to be an opportunity I will cherish and I will take advantage of all the offers to enjoy the festival."

Rubbing his left hand over his completely baldhead, RP said, "I am contented, believe me. I just want to enjoy what is left of my fulfilling life in Elmina and enjoy the company of my family and friends like you."

"I have really enjoyed my visit and I'll certainly be back to see you during the festival," said Mae.

"Please do. You are always welcome."

"Thank you."

After saying good byes and sharing a few jokes with him, the bishop and Mae departed.

*   *   *

At exactly 4.27 on the evening of July 2, 1993, the Ghana Airways flight carrying Jackie, Ama and Bianca touched down at Kotoka International Airport in Accra. The much anticipated first step on the soil of Africa which the children had talked so much about to their friends and classmates was a few minutes away from becoming a reality. Jackie was more excited than the children but she composed herself. When the captain turned off the "Fasten Your Seat Belt" sign for the final time of the journey, Jackie took a deep breath of relief and slowly exhaled her anxiety with her eyes shut in a prayer of thanks. She peered through the window of the plane and for a moment wondered what Ghana had in store for her and the children.

"This is supposed to be home," she thought. "The home I have never known. The home of my ancestors. The home of those great men and women who laid the foundation for me in my adopted land of America. Now I am home and I hope I am welcome. This is the home I want to know intimately and carry with me to America. May my dreams be fulfilled," she prayed.

When Jackie and the children finally disembarked from the plane, she saw a group of other African American tourists who were also visiting Africa for the first time. Many of them were kneeling and kissing the ground and some were shouting with joy for being in Africa. The group, numbering about fifteen belonged to a Baptist church from Boston. They sang a beautiful melodic gospel song, clapped and rattled tambourines as they boarded a bus to the arrival hall. Jackie was equally excited as she joined the singing group to the hall.

The early July weather was cooler than expected as a result of the showers that passed earlier on in the afternoon. The immense heat and humidity that Jackie was expecting to embrace her did not show up. She could feel the excitement in the warm air that blew in their faces. The immigration processing took a short time and within minutes, they were emerging into the customs hall.

"Look at Auntie Mae," exclaimed Bianca who was the first to emerge from the immigration area.

"Where, where, where?" asked Ama.

Before anyone could say another word, they all run to Mae and hugged as she planted kisses on the children. Mae kissed Jackie before turning around to introduce her friends Mr. and Mrs. Cobbinah who accompanied her to the airport.

"How was the journey? Asked Mae.

"Very long," answered Ama.

"Too long," Bianca added.

"Actually it wasn't bad. It was the four and half hour wait in London that frustrated me a bit," Jackie said.

"I prefer the breaks on long journeys."

"I don't know about that."

"Well I am glad that you are here," said Mrs. Cobbinah.

"Thank you," replied Jackie.

The Cobbinahs have been friends of Mae since Mrs. Cobbinah was a student in UCLA in Los Angeles in the late sixties. In fact, in Mae's heart the Cobbinahs were partly the reason she agreed to teach in Ghana for a year.

"This is Ted and his wife Araba. They are my family and very good friends," said Mae as she held Araba. "This is Jackie, her daughter Ama, and my niece Bianca."

They all exchanged greetings in the midst of the hectic activity in the arrival hall as the place filled up with arriving passengers. After the thirteen-hour journey from Dulles Airport through London, the children still had a lot of energy that Mae attributed to excitement. As Ama and Bianca talked to Mae and Araba about their journey, Jackie and Ted wheeled out the luggage.

Minutes later, they had loaded their van and were heading into the heart of Accra. The half hour trip to the suburban home of the Cobbinahs was a new experience for the children, because not only did they see very huge single family homes that looked like mansions but the traffic jam at the height of rush hour on the airport road also reminded them of what they left behind in Baltimore.

When Ted honked the horn of the van, the gates of the house, surrounded by a seven foot white wall started to part exposing the grounds of the five-bedroom house. Ted moved the van unto the grounds and as he eased his six foot four inch frame out of the van, he said, "Akwaaba."

"He means welcome," translated Mae.

"Well, she can speak the language already," Bianca joked.

"Thank you," replied Jackie.

"No, Jackie, you are supposed to say 'Medaase.'"

"What was that again?" asked Jackie.

"Medaase," Mae repeated.

"Medaase, responded the children before Jackie also repeated it.

"Well, it means thank you."

The compound of the Cobbinahs was quite large and the well-lit grounds revealed beautifully manicured lawns. The perimeter of the grounds was lined with huge white flowerpots bearing roses, and in the corners of the garden were beds of marigolds, zinnias and other beautiful flowers. There was a big shrub of fully bloomed Hibiscus in the middle of the grounds and another flowery tree, which Ted referred to as Forget Me Not. The main entrance to the house was concealed behind a roofed porch covered with a well-groomed creeping plant and furnished with white wicker chairs and tables.

With the help of Ted's son and a couple of his friends, the luggage was carried into the house. The warmth of the Cobbinahs was evident from the smiles and the relaxed atmosphere in the house. Ted led the guests into the living room and immediately called his three children to greet their guests. Ama and Bianca focused their eyes on the twelve-year old daughter of the Cobbinahs, Efua, whom they immediately targeted as a playmate.

As the children shook hands with the visitors, Mae asked, "Ted why don't you do your usual thing?"

"Just wait a minute. I want you to relax and have drinks brought out first. Then I'll graciously thank the almighty and our elders for their safe arrival."

"I am anxious to introduce Jackie to our culture."

"Our culture?" Jackie asked.

"Yes, ours."

"Jackie, I must tell you that Mae is a Ghanaian and we shall make you a Ghanaian too before you go back to the

U.S," assured Araba.

"That'll be nice."

"I don't know if three weeks will be sufficient though."

"We'll make the best of it."

"Well, we shall start with the basics," said Ted. And before he finished his sentence, the house help walked in with a tray of soft drinks, beer and bottle of gin. He set the tray on a solid oak table carved into an elephant. Next to the drinks also sat a tray of glasses. Ted poured a short glass of gin and headed for the door leading to the porch. With his seventeen-year old son in tow, he stopped at the door and bowed his head momentarily. He raised the glass of gin above his head and thanked God. He then looked down and started to pour libation in Fante, his native language. He spoke passionately for about two minutes during which he repeatedly poured some of the gin on the ground. He thanked the gods of the area, his ancestors and deceased elders for bringing Jackie and the children safely to Ghana. He prayed for their safety and protection while in Ghana and demanded that the ancestral spirits drive away all evil spirits that could bring harm or any danger to their special guests. He asked for protection for the family and for Mae, and specifically prayed for the guests to return and make Ghana their home. After the libation, he poured a few drops of the gin into the glass, drank it and turned around beaming a broad smile.

"Well spoken, Ted," said Mae.

"Thanks."

"Do you pour libation whenever you have guests?" Jackie asked.

"Only when I get special guests like you."

"Thank you"

"You're welcome."

"Why is that?"

"It also gives me the opportunity to show our culture."

"And I also get to learn a few things when I listen to him," said Mae.

"That's right," replied Ted.

Both Jackie and children knew that Mae did not understand a thing of what Ted said but at least she knew the significance of the libation because they remember her talking about that during one of her slide shows in Baltimore. Araba summarised what Ted said and explained the significance of the libation to Jackie and the children.

"So why don't you pray to God with the drink?" Jackie asked.

"That's a very good question, Jackie. Our custom dictates that you only pray to God with water. Gin, or for that matter any alcoholic beverage is not as pure as water, so you don't offer to God, that which is not pure," explained Ted.

"But I saw you raise the glass to the sky."

"Yes, I did."

"Why?"

"I asked God to bless the drink."

"Then what?" Mae asked.

"Of course, the saying goes that God tells us that whatever we have for him should be given to Mother Earth. That's why we pour the drink on the ground. We offer the drink to Mother Earth before any other spirit or ancestor."

"What's her name, again?"

"Who?" Ted asked.

"Mother earth," responded Jackie.

"Asaase Efua."

"What was that?" Jackie asked again.

"Asaase Efua," Ted repeated.

"That's certainly interesting," said Jackie as she nodded and smiled.

"The seasoned elders who are experts at this will tell you to call the spirits or the elders in the order of their seniority or power," explained Ted.

"There is a whole science to this, right?"

"Oh yes, there is, and I am still learning."

"You seem to be good at it."

"Well, not really."

Ted turned on the stereo, playing soft highlife music while Araba poured drinks for everyone. Shortly after the libation, the twelve-year old daughter of the Cobbinahs took Ama and Bianca out of the living room into the family room where the other children were playing video games. The living room of the Cobbinahs was simply decorated with brown leather sofas, three wooden carved stools, a dimly lit wall unit that housed the stereo system, pieces of wooden and bronze sculptures and other artefacts. There were two huge paintings of an African village at sunset and a market scene on the walls as well as some family pictures. Like any typical upper middle class home in Ghana, the room was also decorated with few potted plants and carvings. As they drank and talked about their plans in Accra before travelling to the university in Cape Coast, Araba vanished into the house and helped to put finishing touches to dinner.

Dinner was chicken stew, fried fish with gravy, rice, boiled yams and kenkey. After a short prayer by Mae, they ate dinner. The children of the Cobbinahs had already had dinner so they continued with their games in the family room. Except for Ama and Bianca who were still full of energy and kept talking to Mae and Ted, Jackie looked very tired and didn't say much at dinner. It was no surprise to anyone when soon after dinner she took a shower, said good night and went to sleep leaving the children with their newly found friends.

Jackie was the first of the guests to wake up in the morning. She quietly took a shower and left the bedroom she was sharing with Ama and Bianca. Araba was also up and reading the morning papers in the living room when Jackie entered.

"Good morning Araba," greeted Jackie.

"Good morning," replied Araba and asked, "Why are you up so early?"

"Have you forgotten that I was the first to go to sleep?"

"Oh yes."

"I think I've had enough sleep."

"You should still be on American time and be sleeping."

"I know. It's about three o'clock in the morning over there."

"That's why you should still be sleeping."

"The children will sleep enough for me. I don't expect them to be up till late."

"Believe me, they will sleep till about mid day because they stayed up late while you slept."

"Good for them. Araba, I must say that you have a beautiful home. I didn't really see how big and beautiful this house was last night."

"Thank you."

"You have a magnificent compound, and I hope you don't mind my looking around."

"Don't be silly, Jackie. Come with me. I'll show you around."

Araba took Jackie through the kitchen to a small vegetable garden behind the house. She pointed out some of the local vegetables that she had grown in the garden and talked about how much she missed the big yards of his father's house when she was growing up. From the vegetable garden, they strolled on to the main grounds where Jackie gravitated to one of the potted rose plants. Araba snapped a yellow rose and handed it over to her saying, "here, this matches your blouse".

"Thank you. It smells good."

"I like them myself."

"How long have you lived here?"

"It's been over ten years now and we are enjoying every bit of this place. It's been a lot of hard work keeping this house the way it is."

"I'm sure."

"Of course we have help from a gentleman who helps with the garden three times a week, but Ted loves to work on the grounds too."

"Where does he find the time to do that?"

"On weekends and on those days when he comes home early. He does a lot to keep the garden the way it is."

"I'd love to have a garden like this in my backyard, but the good Lord knows that I wouldn't be able to maintain it," Jackie said while smelling the rose.

"Oh, I realise how difficult and time consuming it must be to maintain a garden like this in the States. Just reviving the grounds after winter alone must be a lot of work."

"Then one would have to deal with the leaves in the fall also," added Jackie.

"Yes, yes, yes, I know."

"Do you have big trees in your backyard?"

"Thank God, I have only one medium-sized tree. That's one less headache."

"Not much leaves to rake, I guess."

"You got that right."

"I know."

"You are lucky. You don't have to deal with fall and all that cold weather stuff."

"I know."

The two women continued their stroll and settled on the wicker chairs in front of the house. As was usually the case every morning, several birds had gathered on the grounds and were singing. That morning, Araba deliberately ignored the birds and for some strange reason there were a lot more birds than usual.

"Do you raise birds here?" Jackie asked jokingly.

Araba had a good laugh at the question and responded that they were spoiled birds from the neighbourhood that were singing for their food.

"What did you say?"

"It's feeding time."

"You mean you feed the birds?"

"Strange, isn't it?"

"Every day?"

"Yes, every day."

Jackie had a surprising look on her face and didn't understand what Araba meant. However, realising that Jackie was about to ask another question about the birds, she explained how she had followed a practice her mother started when she was a child.

Araba had continued the habit of feeding birds in the morning with boiled rice. The birds usually arrived at about seven o'clock in the morning, sat on the walls and trees and sang for their morning meal. Because of her walk with Jackie, Araba had been late feeding the birds.

Just like her mother, Araba was of the belief that if she fed birds in the morning, they will fly around the neighbourhood and into the city to tell everyone how kind and good the

Cobbinahs are throughout the day. The result of their kindness will be good luck and blessings the birds will bring back to the household the following morning.

"Well it certainly makes sense to me," said Jackie.

"I am not sure about that."

"So how long have you been doing this?"

"Ever since we moved into this house."

"Over ten years?"

"It sounds amazing, doesn't it?"

"You're not kidding. It's amazing."

"When I am not around to feed them, whoever goes to the kitchen first, makes sure that rice is thrown out there behind the vegetable beds for the birds. Maybe this has always brought me good luck."

"I wouldn't be surprised," said Jackie.

"And thank God. I don't have many complaints."

"Thank God," repeated Jackie.

"We're blessed in many ways."

"Well, this means you've got to have boiled rice in the house every day."

"Oh yes, we always do. The fortunate thing is I love rice and wouldn't mind having it every day, so it makes it easier to feed the birds also."

"I love rice too."

"In fact, we cook rice just about every day of the year in this house."

"Wow."

"Wow, indeed."

"Well let's go feed them. Listen to them. They must be hungry."

"I think they are, and possibly mad also," said Araba.

"That's funny."

"I wish I could understand what they are saying."

"I can't wait to see this," said Jackie who anxiously stood up and led the way.

They walked back through the garden to the kitchen as the birds sang louder and louder. Araba scooped a saucer full of rice and threw it on the ground behind the vegetable crops. Within seconds the singing completely ceased as the birds pecked away at the grains.

"This is incredible. I've never seen anything like this in my life," said Jackie who became glued as she leaned on the frame of the kitchen door and watched the birds.

"This is really amazing," she muttered and added, "I hope you bring me lots o'luck during my stay here. You hear me?"

The two women stood there for a while in silence watching the birds eat. Some of the birds that may have had enough started to sing again which Jackie interpreted as their response to her request. She stood out there and continued watching the birds until the last one flew away after every grain had been consumed. And before she turned around to go into the house still holding on to her yellow rose, she whispered, "see you around tomorrow morning."

Mae woke up shortly after the birds had left. She showered and went out for her usual morning walk. When the children woke up and had breakfast, it was past midday. Ted had already left for work, and since Araba worked in a wing of the house as a very successful designer and dressmaker with twelve full time helpers, she had the opportunity to show Jackie and the kids the city of Accra. She gave instructions to her employees and jumped into the Volkswagen van with her guests and her youngest daughter, Efua, and drove off into the city.

"Since you are leaving for Cape Coast tomorrow, this will be a good opportunity to see parts of the city until you come back," said Araba.

"Accra here we come," said Ama who sat in the back seat of the van with Bianca and Efua.

Playing soft highlife music in the background, Araba drove up Achimota Road toward the 37 Military Hospital. While pointing out a few landmarks to Jackie and sometimes the children when she was able to get their attention, she made a remark about the lightness of the traffic on that Saturday afternoon. She took the airport road going in the opposite direction of the airport and headed toward the heart of the city still pointing out all the major buildings and landmarks, foreign embassies and hotels until their steady movement slowed down as they got closer to Makola market, one of the sprawling open markets of the city.

"Jeez, what a huge market," Bianca exclaimed as they drove slowly past the market teeming with thousands of people.

"Is this where you do your shopping, Auntie Araba?" asked Ama.

"No, not really," answered Efua before her mother could respond.

"If we need fresh vegetables, fish and general food items, we usually come to this market or go to others. But if we need frozen food or provisions, we go to the supermarkets," answered Araba.

"Actually, this is like a huge flea market because you can find anything and everything in this market," added Mae.

"Indeed you are right, Mae. That's the best way to describe this market and in fact most markets in Africa."

"Are we going in there to shop?" asked Bianca.

"No, not today."

"So where are we going?" asked Ama.

"I just want you to see how big and active this market is, and then stop over at Zongo Lane to pick up embroidery work being done for some of my clients."

"Sure I remember Zongo Lane," said Mae. "I came here with you to pick up some dresses the last time I was in Ghana."

"Yes, yes, yes, you are right. We are going to see the same guy. He's been working for me for many years and he's very good," said Araba.

"I love his work."

"Oh, he's the best."

"You know, Araba, I haven't seen some of the clothes you make yet. I can't wait to see these ones. I'd love to go back with a whole new wardrobe of African outfits," said Jackie.

"Well, well, the African lady is about to invade Baltimore this summer," joked Mae.

"You bet. I'm going all out."

"We are going all out too," joked Ama.

"Yes, you are also going back with cute dresses."

The traffic in and around the market moved slowly with shoppers and hawkers criss-crossing the busy streets. Many of them seemed not to be in any hurry while others pushed and shoved their way with little patience. After a few minutes of driving through the heart of the market traffic, they approached Zongo Lane.

Zongo Lane was blocked and no vehicles were passing through, so Araba parked the vehicle a block away from where they were going. They all emerged into the heat of the afternoon and started making their way through the busy street. She suspected that there could be a marriage ceremony by the Hausas going on in the area. That and funerals usually caused some street closings on some weekends.

"This could be a wonderful experience for Jackie and the children if it's indeed a wedding," she thought.

"Please be careful as we go up the road because it is very crowded over there. I believe there is a marriage ceremony going on that's why the road is blocked."

"A wedding?" asked Ama and Bianca in unison.

"Yes, but it's not like the type we know in America," said Mae.

"You just wait for a moment, and you'll see," said Araba as she led the group and wove her way through the traffic of humans.

"I hear music," Ama said.

"Yes, there is a party going on."

The drumming, singing and clapping got louder and louder as they got closer to the tailor's workplace.

All of a sudden, they found themselves in the middle of two groups of drummers and scores of dancing and singing women. It was a bit confusing for Araba and her entourage trying to listen to the two dancing groups so Araba asked them to follow her. As they manoeuvred their way from the group on the street toward what appeared to be the main house of the wedding ceremony, the music and the singing started to take on a whole new life.

"Wow, look at all the beautiful outfits of the women," Jackie said.

"This is typical of these women," responded Mae.

"The weddings of the Hausas are beautiful events," added Araba.

"They are different," said Mae.

"They are not like ours at all. You've been to a typical Fante wedding, haven't you?"

"Yes, and they are westernised," answered Mae.

"Well this is a whole new experience."

There were about twenty women in the middle of a circle dancing, singing and thrusting their arms to a steady beat of heavy drums. The rhythm and the lyrics of the song were sweet and harmonious. However, the movement of the women who were dressed in various colourful flowing wraps and gowns with all types and styles of head wraps created the festive atmosphere. The dancing and singing moved the women into a higher crescendo as the drums appeared to sound louder with the steady rhythm of pounding feet.

The music was so good that Araba and her guests stopped their steady progress toward the tailor's shop to enjoy the drumming and the dancing women. They moved closer to the drummers who were seated on a slightly elevated platform that partly blocked the passage to the shop they were heading towards. Then suddenly without any warning Araba joined the dancing of what was certainly an informal wedding. With the children looking on in amazement and embarrassment at Araba, Jackie also melted into the dancing women, pumping her arms in the air and moving with the Hausa women to the beat of the heavy drums. Recognising that Jackie was a foreign tourist in their midst who seemed to be having a good time, a group of the dancing women surrounded her and Araba creating a centre of attraction and urging them to dance on while they clapped, screamed and waved white handkerchiefs to the beat of the music. The circle got tighter and tighter as others poured in. Within seconds there was a huge mass of dancing women bunched up together, thrusting their arms in the air and moving in unison to the pulsating song. This went on for about ten minutes before the drummers faded, leading to a huge applause, more screams and more dust.

Araba and Jackie extricated themselves from the group, hugged and shook hands with some of the women, many of whom knew Araba from her regular visits to the neighbourhood. The women urged Araba and her guests to stay and participate in the celebration but Araba thanked them and politely declined the invitation, citing prior commitments as her reason. The children and Mae who stood by and watched in amazement joined the two uninvited dancers to the tailor who was working in the midst of all the celebration about twenty yards away.

"Araba, I saw you. Ya, ya, ya, you still crazy," said the tailor shaking his head.

"You know something, Abu, you should learn to have fun and relax a little. You work too hard."

"Woman, I have to eat."

"You make enough money to feed all of Accra."

"Who? Me?"

"Yes, you are rich. Just go and join the dancing."

"You funny Araba," replied Abu.

"Abu, these are my friends from America."

"Welcome, welcome."

Abu promptly stood up, bowed to Jackie and Mae and sat down without shaking the outstretched hand of Jackie. He smiled at Jackie and said to Araba, "Explain it to Madam please."

"Explain what?

"Please?" He pleaded.

"Forget about these chauvinist Muslim men. They feel too good to shake a woman's hand," said Araba to the surprised but smiling Jackie.

"Wait a minute, Araba. Do you really mean that Muslim men don't shake hands with women?"

"Well that's what he says."

"No, you're kidding."

"Madam it is true," said one of Abu's colleagues.

"This is interesting."

"I guess so."

"I'm still learning new things," Jackie said, adding, "Mae did you know that?"

"Yes, my dear. I've been around several Muslim men and some shake my hand."

"What do you think?"

"I don't want to shake hands with them either," she joked.

"Oh, Madam," said Abu smiling.

"Abu, please give them your catalogues so they can see some of your work."

"Okay Araba."

Abu opened a glass display case and took out three catalogues.

As Jackie and Mae thumbed through the catalogues the drummers started again in the background and the women rose once again, clapping, singing and dancing. Jackie and Mae selected some of the embroidery designs for outfits to be made later while Araba conducted her business with Abu. Araba collected the dresses Abu had embroidered and once again manoeuvring their way through the marriage festivities; they said good byes to the dancing women and headed into the crowded streets.

"That was fun. It surely feels like a great party," said Jackie.

"It's a big party and it's going to go on 'til late in the night. You must have smelled all the good foods they were cooking in the kitchens. These people know how to celebrate weddings, believe me."

"We didn't even see the bride," said Ama.

"I know," added Bianca.

"She was in the main house."

Bianca asked, "Can we go back?"

"No."

"Why not?"

"Not unless you are ready to dance," replied Araba.

"No way."

"Well then, we are not going back."

"Ok, ok, let's go. I'll dance," said Ama.

"It's too late now," protested Jackie.

"No, that's not fair."

"I'm sorry, my dear, we can't go back now."

"I don't believe this," said Ama.

"Well, better believe it," responded her mother.

Araba led them through the crowded street to the van and took off into the heavy afternoon traffic of hawkers and shoppers. She drove past the central post office building and some of the major shops in the city unto High Street and headed east to the Arts Council for Jackie and Mae to buy some carvings and Kente cloths. Araba played a tourist guide stopping at the old Parliament House and the Kwame Nkrumah Mausoleum to take pictures. They then drove past the government offices to the Black Star Square, where state functions are held and took more pictures. They made a stop at an outdoor restaurant on their way back home after the tour for drinks and snacks before arriving home late in the afternoon.

CHAPTER 4

"Cape Coast University is only two hours from here and the roads aren't bad so we should be there by mid day," said Mae, as they pulled away from the Cobbinahs driveway. With Bianca and Ama still waving to the children of Ted and Araba who were standing in the middle of the quiet street, Mae slowly pulled away from the house.

Their stay in Accra has been short, but to Jackie, that was only the beginning of an exciting visit to a country rich in culture and history. At least, Mae had convinced her of the depth and significance of what the next few days had to offer. History, culture, education and downright understanding and appreciation of their links to Africa. Mae's love for the country was built around the historical significance of slavery, the quest to understand her ancestry which she was convinced was from West Africa and to also understand the cultural significance of her true being.

Driving through the small towns and villages on the way to Cape Coast, Mae pointed out some of the castles and forts built in the fifteenth and sixteenth centuries. She told the children short stories about the country and the local Ghanaians who lived in the coastal towns. She had become very familiar with the Fantes, especially after her visit with the bishop to his friend RP. And to the best of her ability, she imparted her knowledge about the country and its people to the occupants of her car.

"The Fantes are blessed with significant and important history, considering that slavery, early civilisation in West Africa started here and many of the very educated and educators came from these areas."

"I can understand how education started in these areas. These coastal towns are where the white men landed in their boats so any western civilisation or education must have started here," said Jackie.

"I can understand that too," said Ama.

"What?"

"What you just said."

"What did I say?"

"That the white men came to this area first because it's on the coast and they travelled by boats then," answered Bianca.

"That's right."

"So the coastal people, or the Fantes were they first to come into contact with western civilisation," said Ama.

"Well my dear, not all the coastal people are Fantes."

"That's right, Jackie, there are many other tribes along the coast," explained Mae.

"What are tribes?"

"They are a group of people sharing the same culture, language and ancestry."

"Okay."

"Can we be called a tribe?"

"Who is we?" asked Mae.

"African-Americans," answered Ama.

"No. We don't share the same culture. We are too diverse as a group and spread out. Our ancestry may be very different and we don't share the same common values," explained Mae.

"Hmm."

"So all those castles were built by the white people?" asked Bianca.

"Not quite. The local people and slaves helped to build them."

"And you will see and hear more about the history of the white man and the local people several hundred years ago," said Jackie.

"I have written a few poems specifically on slavery but they haven't been published yet," said Mae. "After our visit to the castle in Elmina, I will read you a few. I want the children especially, to appreciate what our ancestors experienced as slaves and how far we've come since those unfortunate, brutal and oppressive days of slavery."

"You mean the slaves came from here?" Ama asked.

"Oh yes my dear, many of our great, great grandfathers and grandmothers came from these shores, and they worked hard in the Americas to make us what we are now," responded Mae.

"That's why you should all pay attention when we visit the castle this afternoon," Jackie said as her eyes met with Bianca's, which caused her to ask.

"Are we going to the castles today?"

"Yes we will go to the Elmina castle this afternoon. Elmina is only fifteen minutes from the university, and I think that's something we could do this afternoon."

"I can't wait," one of the children, said.

"So, Mae what do you really think about slavery and what our ancestors went through. I know how we all feel about it as African Americans, but I haven't really heard you talk much about it except for description of some of the castles and how the slaves were treated and shipped to America.

In fact, most of us don't even think about our ancestry and don't really care. We just take our existence here for granted. Don't we?" asked Jackie peering down her sunglasses.

"Jackie, I get very emotional when I think too deeply about slavery and try to articulate my deep-seated feelings. When I think about the whole process, it makes me feel like my mother was just taken away from me when I was a baby. It's as if I didn't have any mother to nurse me. It's as if I was motherless, fatherless and abandoned. It's as if I was raped, used, abused and when I was finished with, I was sold to someone else who took the last breath of respect and my womanhood from me; then destroyed my identity and forced me to bear his children. I imagine myself in shackles packed in filthy overcrowded, unhygienic, and under the inhumane conditions of a slave ship with hundreds of others. I see myself lying in a pool of urine and faeces for weeks with a daily ration of bread and water, and often times without food for days. I dream about young women and children crying for hours in pain and eventually succumbing to the waiting arms of death after a horrendous fight with the cruelties of life. I cringe with pain at the thought that their young bodies were just flung overboard into the ocean for sharks to feed on. My stomach churns at the thought of the cruelty and the lack of respect for human life. A life that I define as the dreams and wishes of man, by man, for the disadvantaged and the powerless. I mean sheer cruelty. Cruelty, my dear. All in the name of what? Money, ignorance and greed?"

"Money and ignorance?" asked Jackie.

"Oh yes, my dear. One of these days we will do an in-depth analysis, just by reasoning. We shall forget about the books and what others thought. We will try to figure out everything by ourselves and the children will be part of it."

"That will be good."

Mae paused for a moment, took a deep breath when she was about to be overcome with emotion and continued.

"I look at life and wonder how far we've come from such cruel treatments and try to find justification for the suffering and misery. But I usually find myself chasing my own tail. I find myself drowning in confusion and in inexplicable nightmares. I have read a lot about slavery. I tried to place myself in the minds of those who sold their own kind into slavery, and while I have found answers to some of their actions, I have not been able to confront the evils of the white man that melted away generations of families and perpetuated the evil practice of slavery."

"I hear you" Jackie interjected.

"Girl, I have not been able to understand man as an entity then and even now, and I may never do. That's one aspect of slavery that I am still trying to understand - Man. And the more I think about it, the more I realise that man and evil are such complex entities and destructive forces which only the divine Father can understand. We have come a long way from the days when we could be bought and sold. But Girl, we are still a long way from home and dignity. The sun hasn't shone on us yet. Maybe we have blocked out the rays of hope by our own actions and deeds. Maybe we have condemned our own race through apathy, ignorance, selfishness and the lack of resolve to uplift our spirits. Maybe we have designed and chartered the course of our lives into complete disrepair. Can we blame the white man?"

"Yes we can," answered Jackie.

"But, to what extent? To some extent of course, but we cannot dump every blame on him. We are our own men and women. We are our own persons and families. We are our own nation. And what have we done to move the person, family or nation forward? What have we done, Jackie? Nothing. Nothing. Indeed, nothing of significance. We have a long road ahead of us, and believe me it is going to be rough and extremely painful travelling that road."

"It's amazing what powers we have and what we have not been able to do," interrupted Jackie.

"It is amazing, my dear."

"And rather sad."

There was silence in the car for a moment as they tried to appreciate what Mae had just talked about in preparation for their visit to the castles. Even the children remained still and everyone seemed to be deeply in thought.

Mae interrupted her feelings and started to slow down the car when she saw fruits and vegetables being sold on the roadside. The oranges, bananas and pineapples had been arranged beautifully on tables and in big trays that were delicately balanced on the heads of the children and women selling them.

She brought the car to a stop and that also interrupted Jackie's deep thoughts. They filled the car with fruits, ate some and joked with the children hawking the fruits.

When they resumed their journey, Jackie made a remark about how the African American man has not contributed much to uplift the image of the Black man, especially in the inner cities. Before she could continue further, Mae interrupted and started talking about one of the greatest Ghanaians she admired.

"Jackie, you just reminded me of this great Fante man who came to America in the early nineteen hundreds. His name was J.E.K. Aggrey."

"Who's he?"

"What you just said about African American young men letting us down reminded me of the tremendous work our black leaders and in fact, families must do to turn this generation around. We are heading toward a major disaster that will consume a whole generation of young men if we don't act quickly and effectively. Do you know what Dr. Aggrey said when he realised the shortcomings of our race?"

"What?" asked Ama.

"He said, if he went to heaven and God said to him that he was sending him back to earth as a white man what would he do? He said that, he will plead with God to send him back as black as he could make him. And if God asked him why, he would answer that, no white man can do the work that he's going to do as a black man. No white man understands our culture and thinks like us. The white man does not appreciate our problems and our suffering. So how can he solve the problems that he doesn't understand?"

"That makes sense," said Jackie.

"Darling, this really means that no government or politician is going to solve the problems of the African American or the black man for us. They will travel to all the ghettos, Harlems, East LA's and all those rundown places and promise salvation and heaven, but if we don't recognise ourselves that we have major problems and find solutions to them, our own solutions, we are doomed. Doomed and doomed to perish in our own debacle. The black male in America will become a fifth class citizen in a fourth class neighbourhood in a third class country because the ripple effects will reach beyond every pocket and corner of the country. And that will affect every man and woman in the country."

"Really?" Ama Asked.

"Yes, really."

"We are seeing that right now, Mae. What kind of students are we producing in many of the inner-city public schools? What kind of children are we bringing up in the neighbourhoods? You know what? It is scary, very scary. Those that manage to stay alive from drugs and the senseless killing and carnage in the cities are ending up in prisons. It's so pathetic that it is frightening," said Jackie as they approached the outskirts of Cape Coast.

"One can never finish talking about the problems of the young African American male today," said Mae.

"We can't leave out the females either."

"Oh girl, ain't that right?"

"We live in a world where the core of the family is non-existent."

"Sadly so, Jackie."

"It's an enormous problem, whose solution may sadly emerge from the destruction of a whole generation."

"The thought saddens me, but there is still hope," said Mae, and added "we are on the outskirts of Cape Coast and only ten minutes from the university."

The children were amazed at the size of the campus as they entered the university from the eastern entrance. Mae drove past the massive buildings of Volta and Casley Hayford Halls into the heart of the campus. She entered the grounds of the science faculty complex and showed them some of the beautiful architectural pieces of the campus before heading up the hills to her three-bedroom bungalow.

"The campus is beautiful", said Jackie.

"I fell in love with the campus too when I first came here. It's really pretty and modern. However, I tend to prefer the architecture and layout of the campus of University of Ghana in Accra."

"We'll see that campus too. Right?"

"Of course we will when we go back to Accra."

"Are the students on vacation?" asked Ama.

"Yes my dear, that's why the campus is so quiet. I believe they will be back in September," said Mae as she pulled into the driveway of her bungalow.

"Mae, you have such a wonderful view. My goodness, this is pretty. Look at the ocean and the coconut trees. This must be very relaxing in the evenings," Jackie said.

"I love this place already," Ama screamed.

"Keep it down Ama," said Bianca.

"Shall we go to the beach?"

"Not now, my dear."

"Wait till you see the rising sun from behind the coconut trees in the early morning."

"I can just imagine it," said Jackie as she focused her camera to take pictures of the scenic view.

Jackie took a couple of pictures of the coconut tree-lined beaches before helping to unload the car. Mae showed the children to their room and Jackie to her room. After a lunch of tuna salad sandwiches, juicy pineapples and iced tea on the front porch of the house with a view of the ocean, they climbed back into the car and headed west toward Elmina.

As they approached Elmina, Mae told them a brief history of the ancient fishing town and the people who lived in it. She drove through the famous quaint town pointing out some landmarks she learned from her previous visits. The roads were very busy and crowded with thousands of visitors and tourists who had arrived for the annual Bakatue Festival. Mae was not quite sure about her knowledge of the festival so she deferred the story to the tour guide she hoped they would meet at the castle. Slowly, she made her way through the crowded narrow streets that had been decorated with colourful flags and banners. She drove across the bridge on the Benya River to the castle and parked among tourist buses and several other cars. They took pictures of the castle and the fort overlooking the castle about a quarter of a mile away before making their way toward the castle.

"Wow, this town is really busy," said Ama.

"I hope it's not this crowded in the castle," added Bianca.

"It's like a street fair."

"I don't think so," responded Mae. "The festival is usually big and if you think this is a huge crowd, wait till tomorrow."

"We'll see it, right?" Ama asked.

"Oh yes," Jackie assured.

"I understand tomorrow is the grand finale of the festival with all kinds of activities along the river. We will try to get close to the river to see the boat races, the pageantry and parade of chiefs and various other activities tomorrow," Mae seemed to assure Ama.

"Believe me, we'll be here early," Jackie concurred.

"Well, let's try to get a lot out of today," said Mae as they approached the castle.

There was a guided tour about to begin at the main gate as they entered the castle, so they joined the group.

The afternoon breeze from the ocean was refreshing and humidity was low. Jackie was wearing tightly fitted jeans and a red T-shirt with the inscription "I'm from Elmina" on the front, "…and proud of it" on the back. Mae had purchased the shirt for her a week earlier. Ama and Bianca were also in shorts and T-shirts while Mae wore a loose African outfit. With her hair pulled back and wearing sunglasses, Jackie's beauty caused almost all those who saw her to take a second look. She looked stunningly attractive that afternoon.

They managed to secure good positions among the tourists before the tour guide made his way to the group. The group of about twenty people made up of primarily tourists from Europe and the United States of America focused on the six-foot partly bald tour guide who appeared to be in his early forties. Franco had a decent potbelly that was miniaturised by his height. He was a good-looking man though but it was his deep rich voice that attracted attention.

The guide made a cursory survey of the group and greeted in a somewhat British accent, "Good afternoon ladies and gentlemen."

"Good afternoon," responded the group in unison.

"My name is Franco Ammisah and I will be your guide for this tour. First of all, let me welcome you to this castle on behalf of the Omanhene of Elmina, the Museum and Monuments Board of Ghana and the people of Elmina of which I am one and of course, the lady in the red T-shirt", referring to Jackie who shot back a smile. "As you know, tomorrow is the big festival. The Bakatue festival, and I don't expect to tell you much about it this afternoon."

"Why not?" asked an elderly French lady who looked to be in her late sixties.

"Well, this tour will focus on the castle, but I will also try and tell you briefly about the festival and answer any questions you have. Will that be all right?"

"Yes. Thank you, Franco," the lady said with a smile.

"You're welcome."

"Before we enter the castle, could you please follow me this way?" he asked, and led them to a rectangular structure in front of the castle.

The tourists followed him to and stood around a

rectangular structure which he described as what the Portuguese and Dutch navigators used to set their compasses before going on journeys.

"In fact Christopher Columbus was in this town several years before he set sail for the Americas. He set his compass here on one of his journeys across the seas. Well, I hope the Americans among us realise how important and significant this castle is," said Franco. "At least Elmina could be a footnote in the history of how the homeland of the Americans was discovered."

With that, he turned around and like a faithful flock, the tourists followed him toward the entrance of the castle. As they entered, he turned and said, "This castle is the oldest structure built by the Europeans in tropical Africa. It was built by the Portuguese in 1482. When the Portuguese arrived here in the early fourteen hundreds, they were amazed at how much gold the inhabitants and the area had. As a result, they named this town 'A Mina' or The Mine."

Crossing the drawbridge leading into the castle, Franco stopped in the middle and said, "Let me tell you a brief history about who and how the castle was built before we go in. This way, I can show and tell you about the various parts of the building without focusing on the history of the entire building."

"Okay," someone said.

"You see, King John III of Portugal ordered the building of this castle by Don Diego da Azambuja. Don Diego commanded the first men who settled here and built the castle. He came here with hundreds of masons, carpenters, artisans and over five hundred soldiers to protect them. They came here with tons of building materials including cut stones, tiles, gates, lime, nails, timber and several tools.

Some people even believe that the Portuguese came with prefabricated materials but that is disputed by historians."

"So, how many of them came here in the beginning?" asked the elderly French woman.

"I will say about one thousand men and a few women."

"And how long did it take to build it?" an European lady who also sounded French asked.

"Well, that is difficult to tell, but the Portuguese built it very quickly. Especially the walls surrounding the castle which took only about twenty-eight days to complete."

"Twenty-eight days?" asked one of the tourists.

"Yes, only twenty-eight days."

"Jeeez, that was a major accomplishment, considering how long it takes some of our construction people to fix a kitchen," the woman said as people laughed.

"Yes they had to build it quickly."

"Why?"

"They had no choice. This is because the inhabitants had fought them and prevented them from carving out one of the biggest rocks on the land, which they considered sacred. So having fought off the inhabitants a few times, they had to quickly build the walls around the castle for protection."

"Before I continue, I want all of you to turn around and take a look at the fort on that hill overlooking the castle," said Franco pointing northward.

All the tourists turned and looked at the fort that looked rather small compared to the castle.

"That is Fort St. Jago, and I will tell you about it as we go along."

"Was that also built by the Portuguese?" asked one of the Europeans.

"No, that was built by the Dutch."

"In any case," continued Franco, "the presence of the castle allowed the Portuguese to keep a strong military presence in this area and in Africa in general. Since they were the first here, they monopolised the gold and the trade, and considered all other nationalities that came to the area as pirates. In fact, they seized or destroyed their ships and some of the sailors were believed to have even been executed. The Portuguese controlled the Gold Coast for several years until the Dutch established a beachhead in a town called Moree, which is about 25 miles away. They traded with the inhabitants there for years, and at an opportune time, decided to attack the Portuguese here. Everyone wanted the castle and the power it presented. It took the Dutch three attempts before they were able to capture this castle. They attacked the Portuguese from the hill up there where the fort stands. They attacked with cannons and mortars until the Portuguese surrendered in 1627. The Dutch were a determined people," he said, as he blotted off beads of sweat from his forehead.

"The Dutch also fortified the castle against attacks and built Fort St. Jago on the hill," pointing in the direction of the fort, "to protect the castle from enemies from the sea and also land. They moved heavy canons to vantage points and that strengthened their positions in the castle."

After talking about the surrender of the castle by the Portuguese, he spoke about the other security devices used then. He explained the purpose of the drawbridge and that of the inner and outer walls of the castle as additional protective devices which could be flooded with sea water to protect against attacks. The tour guide turned around and headed into the inner courtyard of the castle after a brief lecture on the bridge and the moats. Franco came to a stop in the great courtyard and gave a short speech on the significance of the castle with respect to slavery and the slave trade.

The mention of slavery heightened the anxiety of Jackie who had a sick feeling in her stomach. This is the closest she had come to experiencing how the slaves lived and how they were treated in Africa. She made a mental note to pay close attention to the guide. Franco led them to the cold dark rooms on the southern sections of the yard where the male slaves were held and brought them back to the courtyard to show them a dry well into which the difficult and trouble-making male slaves were thrown.

"Do you mean the slaves were literally thrown into the wells?" asked Jackie, elbowing her way to the front of the group to have a closer look of the well.

"Yes."

"Really?"

"Yes, Madam. They were dropped in there like rocks. Many of them suffered broken bones from the fall into the wells. They were only brought out when the slave ships arrived to take them away. Those who died from their wounds were taken out and buried. But let me say that the slave masters liked that, because even though the slaves were in chains, they feared trouble at sea during the long journeys across the Atlantic."

He showed them the Portuguese church on the court, the batteries on the eastern section of the castle and led them to the Prempeh room.

"This room is very important to the Asantes because this is where the King of the Asante's, Prempeh the First was held by the British before being exiled to the Seychelles Islands. The islands are in the Indian Ocean, east of Tanzania. You know, ladies and gentlemen, the British and the Asantes fought many wars and did not trust each other. During one of their encounters, the British demanded what is believed to be the soul of the Asante nation, the Golden Stool. The Asante king refused to give up the stool and obviously the soul of the Asante nation, and this resulted in a war between the British and the Asantes. Led by a fiery woman called Yaa Asantewa, they fought the British troops and never gave up the stool and many other state treasures that the British were seeking. As a result, the king was captured and brought here."

"All the way from Kumasi?" asked the elderly French woman.

"Yes. They kept him here before he was exiled."

"Talk about arrogance," Jackie whispered.

"And greed," concurred Mae.

With that brief lecture, Franco led the group to the governor's quarters and the section where the female slaves were kept. They toured the bedrooms, offices, kitchen, dining room and the shop before ending up in the female slave quarters.

"Mae, this is very depressing," said Jackie.

"The conditions here were bad, but the dungeons I saw in the Cape Coast castle are worse," responded Mae.

"Do you know something?"

"What?"

"I have a strange feeling that I've seen this place before, and it gives me an awful feeling," said Jackie.

"Maa, I feel funny too."

"I wouldn't wish these living hell conditions on anyone," whispered Mae.

"That's right."

"I wish our fellow brothers and sisters will come down here to see the cruelties and degrading treatment the slaves endured so they will appreciate life and make something out of themselves," Mae whispered again, as she held her niece's hand tightly.

"It just looks like we've gone from the chains of human slavery to the chains of economic slavery, social and moral decay and complete disintegration of our family values in America," said Jackie, holding on to her daughter tightly as if she was protecting her from being snatched away.

Just when Jackie was beginning to sink her emotions deeply into the life of the slaves, the guide drew their attention to a window-like opening that the governors and the senior slave masters looked through to see what was going on in the female slave quarters.

"The slave masters also used the window to select the slaves they found attractive or liked to sleep with," Franco said.

"What else is new with men?" whispered Jackie.

"They are all the same," Mae agreed.

Moving into another room adjacent to the governor's kitchen, Franco's deep voice echoed through the tiny room. "When the masters see a woman they liked, the guards would bring her into this room, give her a good bath and prepare her for the governor or whomever to sleep with. Of course, many of the slaves became pregnant and had children of the slave masters."

"That's very sickening," whispered Jackie.

"It happened in America too," said Mae.

"If you go into town, and in fact to many of the coastal towns in Ghana, you will see many fair coloured people and families with Portuguese and Dutch names, and some of these are descendants of the European slave masters."

"Were the pregnant women also transported in slave

ships?"

"Usually, the pregnant women were set free and housed outside the castle. Here in Elmina, there are many families with Dutch and Portuguese ancestry, and I am one of them." He smiled to the tourists and said, "Thank you for coming."

With that remark which was his standard closing remark of every tour, he asked if any of the tourists had questions. After a few questions and answers, he showed them the gift shop and led some of them back into the great court and invited them to look around.

Mae and Jackie returned to the governor's quarters with the children in tow to look around. They seemed to have unfinished business in the governor's quarters. Leaning on the wall overlooking the female slave quarters, Jackie went into a reverie. For that short moment that she rested her body on the wall, she was consumed by centuries of time. She heard a distant voice calling her, "Nana Yaa, Nana Yaa."

She tried to answer but she felt too tired and weak. Her lips were too dry to even muster an answer to her name.

"Nana Yaa, Nana Yaa," she heard the voice again coming from the bushes behind her room but she could not answer. She could hear and feel thousands of feet stampeding toward her. She saw several familiar faces and strange faces. Many of the faces looked scary and white. She seemed rooted to her place and could not run. Her mind told her to get up and run to stay ahead of the stampeding people but she could not move. All of a sudden she felt a pair of cold hands lifting her up. It felt like a welcome feeling so she did not panic. She gradually turned around but saw no one. Suddenly the voice calling her name became louder. The voice told her to get up and run, but try as she did, she felt like she was being swallowed by a huge sinkhole. Then fear started to well up n her as the stampeding people caught up with her. She was overwhelmed by the hundreds of people running over her and kicking her. She began to lose consciousness. Then suddenly she woke up in sweat and breathing heavily.

*   *   *

The morning sun had not pierced through the hut with its powerful rays as was usually the case to get her up from bed. However, the pace of activities in the courtyard seemed vigorous enough to tell her that the morning was going to be an unusual one. It was still dawn. The courtyard of the chief of Kumadu usually comes to life very early in the morning with servants preparing the early morning meals, hunters setting out for the morning hunt and farmers getting an early start to beat the sun. The courtyard contained twenty homes, well constructed with bamboo, wood and mud. Being the palace of the chief, the complex was elegant and was surrounded by a thick fence made of bamboo and wood. All the buildings on the compound were round in structure and the chief's house stood out as the biggest. The twenty brown buildings were arranged in circular form and the entrances opened into a big courtyard with three huge mahogany trees and other smaller trees. The grounds were always cleanly maintained and littering was not tolerated. Cleanliness was ingrained even in the children.

The chief of Kumadu, Nana Kofi Amankwatia Poku, was a very powerful man with significant influence in the affairs of the eight surrounding villages he governed. Being Asantes, Nana Poku and his subjects still paid allegiance to the Asante King and his stool. Nevertheless, he considered himself a powerful chief in his own right because of the rich resources of gold he controlled in his domain. He was well-respected by the elders of the eight villages he had jurisdiction over, simply because of his wealth. Besides, he was a legendary war tactician and a brave man revered in the Asante nation. He was the brain behind the strategies of the wars won by the powerful Asante armies. As a result of his legendary bravery, his courtyard was almost always filled with warriors and elders making plans to defend their rich resources from possible invading forces.

Nana Poku was aware of his power and influence in the kingdom, but the most important thing on his mind was the only daughter he had among his ten children. In his mind, Nana Yaa was the most beautiful woman on earth. Indeed, she was. Standing five feet ten inches, Nana Yaa was an imposing woman, because she not only turned the heads of the most powerful chiefs in the kingdom, she was the most sought after woman by the richest men. Nana Yaa had all the features of a great queen, but the natural power of her beauty and wisdom, which many believe she inherited from her father, made her the envy of the powerful men in the Asante kingdom. Being a woman, her father did not actively consult with her in public on major issues. However, in the privacy of his room, Nana Poku relied on the advice of his daughter. In fact, the very close elders in the courts of the chief knew how much Nana Poku depended on his thirty-year-old daughter.

Soon after the first crow of the rooster, the heavy drums in Nana Poku's courtyard sounded. The distinct sounds of the war drums were very different from what the villagers were normally used to. The drumming had started earlier than normal and that signified an unusual occurrence. The elders of the village certainly knew the significance and meaning of the message of the drummers, and the fact that it preceded the first light of the day meant the chief was already up and working.

In various outfits and red dyed cloths, the elders entered the courtyard of Nana Poku. The early dawn had become alive with flaming torches and small fires in the courtyard. Unlike Nana Poku who was wide awake and was in his room with his chief linguist and some of his grown sons, all the elders who arrived looked sleepy and seemed to drag themselves into the courtyard. Nana Yaa heard the drums and knew the meaning but did not get up. She knew the significance of the war drums and was aware that there were serious issues to be discussed. She was astute enough to realise that it was too early to walk into the courtyard with all the elders gathered. She would be out of place being the only woman among the elders. Besides, she was not officially considered an advisor to the chief or a war general so she stayed in bed and waited for her father's summons.

Nana Yaa stayed in her room for over two hours wondering what was going on in the courtyard. The powerful rays of the sun had started to penetrate the windows of her hut. She could hear the voices of the elders but they were not clear enough for her to discern the substance of the discussions. She knew that it was only a matter of time when her father would summon her. As she waited, minutes seemed like hours and her anxiety caused her heart to start thumping. "There must be some thing very wrong she kept thinking." She thought about the worst and about the death of the King of Asante and what that would mean to her father. But she figured that if the king was dead, his father would not be meeting with the elders for that long. Rather, he would be on his way to Kumasi.

With several scenarios running at top speed through her head, Nana Yaa did not hear the knock on her door. When the servant knocked on her door the second time, she dragged herself from bed completely drained by anxiety. The servant informed her that she was wanted urgently by her father. Chewing a fibrous sponge quickly to clean her teeth, Nana Yaa hurriedly washed her face, tied on a red cloth above her chest and emerged from her hut. The courtyard was filled with war generals and other divisional chiefs. There were some men sitting near fires and working on tools while others just sat in groups and talked. The courtyard had been swept clean and the women and children were in their quarters not interfering with the gathering of the elders.

Nana Yaa walked across the courtyard to the gaze of all the elders and chiefs to her father's quarters. She bowed and greeted the elders who had assembled in the courtyard and gracefully entered the room leading to her father's bedroom. In the bedroom were four of her brothers and their father. The gathering was unusual that morning. Walking through the courtyard, she sensed that there could be trouble brewing when she saw some of the senior warriors that early in the morning.

"Maakye Nana," she greeted her father.

"Yaa oheneba," he responded.

She then greeted her brothers, but unlike their father they did not usually respond to her as princess. Nevertheless, before her brothers could respond to their sister's greeting, Nana Poku beckoned her to sit. Nana Yaa was a very confident woman with an explosive temper. She could not tolerate laziness, incompetence and lies. Many men made an extra effort not to offend her because of her temper. She was well-versed in the affairs of the state and some of the elders even consulted with her. She was, respectful and never disobedient to her father or any of the town's elders.

For the second time in three weeks, Nana Poku had been warned by his intelligence staff of an impending British attack. All the villages had been on alert for weeks but nothing had happened. Nana Poku spoke with his children to develop strategies, should the kingdom be attacked. He was a practical man who was aware that the enemy knew of his power, wealth and legendary warfare skills and would try to kill or capture him given the slightest opportunity. Consulting with his sons who were also good warriors and in fact, captains of his armies, the family members formulated a strategy to present to the elders and army captains.

As he always cautioned, he reminded the most important person in his life, her princess Nana Yaa, not to venture out to the war front no matter what happened. He was aware of his daughter's love for him and her temper, which could cause her to avenge his death on the British if he were to be captured or killed in a war against them. He warned his sons to ensure their sister's safety in the event of an attack. Alternate plans for escape were made and all the arrangements and agreements they made amongst the family members were sealed with their father's blessing. He poured libation, said a short prayer to his ancestors and dismissed his children.

The morning sun shone brighter and the day had started becoming hot already. There was a lot of activity in the courtyard as servants arranged chairs under a mahogany tree in the middle of the courtyard. After meeting with his children in the privacy of his quarters, Nana Poku emerged to meet again with the elders. When they had all taken their seats, the chief linguist called the meeting to order. He poured libation to the gods of the land before the chief spoke. They discussed the impending attack, made their battle plans and assigned responsibilities to the war captains and elders of the villages. The two-hour meeting culminated with a big meal prepared by several women who had been cooking in a section of the courtyard all morning.

"Could this be the last meal we will have together as one big powerful and rich family," Nana Poku asked his chief linguist and trusted confidant.

The elder assured his chief that the British did not have the discipline to fight the Asante army. He reminded Nana Poku of his wisdom, his successes against other powerful fighting forces and the fear his name created among opposing armies. He assured his leader that their army was only a section of a bigger force that was ready to defend the nation. Indeed, the three army divisions that Nana Poku controlled was only a section of the forces that were poised to defend the pride and treasures of the nation. However, Nana Poku did not have complete control of the entire army, and even though he was the focal point of many of the strategy meetings, he had an unusual feeling that something would not go right.

Even though the words of the elders seemed to comfort and assure him, he was not truly convinced that the nation was well prepared to face the well-armed British forces that his scouts had warned were advancing, but were several days away. As confident and powerful as he was, Nana Poku had an uncomfortable feeling that this war unlike the previous wars would be different. He knew from his scouts that the British were heavily armed this time to avenge their defeat in the battle of Nsuta. He worried about the possible outcome but he could not put his finger on the factors that would determine the outcome of the war. It was that feeling of uncertainty that had caused him to bring his children together again to develop a family strategy for the war after the general meeting of the elders and war captains.

As darkness descended on the village and shadows began to melt into the evening, Nana Poku resigned himself to fate. He had dinner with his daughter alone in his quarters and gave her specific instructions as to what she should do if he died or was captured. Later, he spent the evening listening to children sing and play in the courtyard with his daughter. He enjoyed the games and songs his princess taught the children and reminisced about the wonderful life he enjoyed as a chief, his riches, power and the respect he enjoyed as the best tactician and warrior in the nation. He thanked the gods for the most precious gift of all, Nana Yaa, and beamed a confident smile when her sweet voice rose and penetrated the falling darkness to strike a chord in his heart. To him, that was life. That was what he lived for. Deep down in his heart, he was satisfied with life and was ready to move on if he died in the inevitable war with the British.

He slowly stood up and walked gracefully into his hut as the voice of his princess faded and melted into the darkness of his room.

*   *   *

Her legs were very sore. Her arms ached and her muscles were still stiff from the three-day journey to the coast after her capture by the British soldiers. Nana Yaa had refused to eat for three days and all the women in the slave quarters had become concerned. She was a stubborn and proud woman and was determined to make her anger felt. Even though she wasn't sure to whom her anger was directed, the hurt and irritated temper prevented her from rationalising her predicament. Her heart bled and she felt lost. The thought of losing her family and father created a mixed emotion of anger and hurt. The confused state of her mind caused her to spit on one of the British guards on her arrival at the castle. An act for which she received a severe whipping. The other slaves were realistic enough to recognise that in their situation as slaves, they could not do anything to stop the ill treatment they were receiving, as painful and humiliated as they felt. Besides, there was nowhere else to turn and the hopelessness of their situation was evidenced by the huge walls and steel gates that surrounded them.

The rooms the slaves were held were damp and cold. The air was stale and no one spoke. The looks on their faces confirmed the hopelessness of the situation. Proud and powerful warriors including royalty had now been reduced to slaves in waiting. Waiting for their fate to be determined by strange white-skinned men they could not understand, let alone reason with.

Sitting in a corner of the room that housed about fifty other slaves, Nana Yaa regretted not having listened to her father. As the only daughter, she had been warned not to set foot outside the courtyard but to leave the village with an assigned group and go into hiding during the war.

She thought hard about her father's love and desire to give her the best. She thought about all the privileges and the power she enjoyed because of her father. When she realised that life was going to be different from that day forward, and that her family was lost, tears started to flow down her face. For the first time she felt vulnerable. Her temper and strong will had landed her in her present predicament. She had accompanied the warriors to the outskirts of town the night before the advanced scouts had predicted the British attack. But in a surprise move, the British attacked a day earlier than anticipated. The resulting massacre and defeat of the Kumadu people also led to Nana Yaa's capture on the battlefield.

Overwhelmed by hunger for the past three days, Nana Yaa felt weak. Still sitting on the floor in a corner, she drifted into a fitful sleep. Word had reached the governor about her outstanding rudeness and stubborn attitude. Strong traits and pride, which according to the guards, masked her beauty. Her dark chocolate complexion and huge brown eyes that seemed to pierce the hearts of men had lost its lustre in the slave quarters. The full lips that sang the most beautiful songs in her father's courtyard were now dry and parched. Even in her half naked, hungry and dirty condition, she still radiated the special qualities of a beautiful woman. But, she was a broken woman.

Nana Yaa was awakened by one of the guards from the corner of the room, which she had occupied with other slaves since arriving at the castle. She was helped to an adjoining room of the governor's kitchen. With the help of another female slave, she had her first bath in a week and was dressed in a long loose-fitting dress. After a brief lecture from the woman who had helped to clean her up, she ate some food. Sitting in the room by herself, she wondered why she had been singled out, given a bath and clothed. She was too drained to think rationally, but the situation was totally unexpected so she struggled to engage her mind.

"Why are they doing this to me? Are they doing this because I am a princess?" she wondered. "I am still a slave. I have been disgraced. I have been stubborn and have not listened to my father. Why am I here? Am I going to be exchanged for some captured white soldiers? I want to go home. I don't belong here, I don't belong here," she cried silently.

As these thoughts zipped through her head, one of the governor's servants appeared in the doorway. The servant beckoned her to follow him. She complied without any protest and after going through the kitchen and the dining room, entered the governor's living room. The room was well decorated with beautiful furniture and artefacts. It became clear to Nana Yaa that many of the gold artefacts were stolen from the Asante villages after the wars.

She was left standing there by herself for a while before the governor appeared in the doorway dressed to intimidate in his full regalia. The white man stood about three, maybe four inches taller than Nana Yaa. He had a full beard with strands of gray even though he could not be older than fifty years. He surveyed the woman over and motioned her to come to him. For a moment, Nana Yaa froze in place not knowing what to do in a room alone with a white man. As the governor motioned her to approach him for the second time, she took a few steps out of fear and then stopped. Running out of patience, the governor moved forward and snatched the slave's hand. She screamed and pulled herself free examining her arm to see if the white man's colour had rubbed off on her. She held her hands tightly close to her chest and waited for the governor to move forward. Her heart was pumping rapidly and beads of sweat had started forming on her forehead. As the governor moved again toward her, she slowly slid down and sat on the floor burying her head in between her legs and covering her head with both hands. She started to tremble as fear began to well up in her. She stayed in that position with the governor looking over her and muttering to himself. After a few minutes, he left the slave there and retreated into his bedroom.

The sun finally set over the hill to the west of the castle. Darkness slowly consumed the castle, and Nana Yaa still sat on the floor of the governor's private room. Seventy-five minutes had seemed like an entire night to the slave. The room had gradually grown darker by the minute. The fear that had usually accompanied darkness since her arrival at the castle wasn't there anymore. The seventy-five minutes by herself in the governor's quarters had given her time to reflect on the uselessness and hopelessness of the situation.

"They were right not to fight the guards," she thought to herself about the other female slaves. She had convinced herself that the strange white man could not harm her. She had gradually but reluctantly accepted her predicament. However, she had made a commitment to herself to uphold her integrity and was determined to fight any physical abuse. Thinking that she was a princess and must use her position to advance the cause of her female slaves, she sat up straight as the flickering flames of a lantern approached the room.

"After all, the worst will be death. I have lost my family. I have lost my father and don't have anything to live for. I am prepared now, more than ever to fight to death," she said to herself.

When the governor's servant emerged from the shadows, she stood up with a pouted mouth in the dark. The servant motioned her to follow him, which she readily did. She was led to the room adjacent to the kitchen where she was initially prepared prior to her encounter with the governor. For the next seven days, she stayed in that room with two other slaves including the woman who had helped prepare her to meet the governor. Life in the governor's quarters was light years away from life in the slave quarters where the women were strewn on the cold floor with little food and no clothing on most of them. She felt uncomfortable whenever she thought about the other slaves but she resigned herself to the fact that there was nothing she could do to help them at that moment. As the influence of the other three privileged slaves in her room began to overtake her principles and beliefs, she felt more relaxed in their company. She had realised that the women were sleeping with the governor or some of the other white men. Initially she found that to be appalling but as time passed, she softened her tone of condemnation realising that the women were trying to make lives better for themselves as super-slaves or trying to gain their freedom.

On the evening of the eighth day, Nana Yaa was once again taken into the governor's quarters. The other three women who shared her room had been called away earlier on. Waiting in the same room she had waited eight days earlier, the governor emerged from the shadows. It was dark, except for a small lantern, which flickered atop a table near the door from where the governor emerged. His shadow was long and his long beard added another six inches to his chin. Nana Yaa studied the shadow and as strange and ghostly as it seemed, she remained calm. Unlike her previous experience, the fear of the approaching white man had disappeared. She thanked the gods for hiding his strange white colour in the dark. Closing her eyes as he stood in front of her, she felt his cold hands on her arm. She froze immediately and withdrew her arm. The governor also retreated for a moment wondering if he had to adopt a new strategy to entice his prey. He tried again, and this time he held her arm firmly and gently pulled her. Trying not to resist, she slowly followed the governor out of the room.

The governor's bedroom was dimly lit by a small lantern that sat on a table next to his bed. Still holding on to the slave, he led her to the edge of the bed. He sat down on the edge of the bed and tried to force Nana Yaa to sit down also but she refused. Slowly, he worked his hands on the hips of the slave and tried to pull up the long dress she wore. The thought of the white man about to invade her body frightened her and caused her to freeze in fear. She stood there shivering and praying silently. Gradually, the governor lifted her dress as she still stood near the bed. Then in a flash, he flipped the slave unto the bed like a light rag doll. As soon as Nana Yaa hit the bed, she bounced off like a tennis ball and stood back up next to the bed. She assumed her old stiff posture and stared down at the governor who was still sitting. He grabbed the slave by the hand again, and forced her on the bed cursing in English. She responded in her native language in protest to be left alone as her anger welled up. As the dialogue in the two languages raged on amid the struggle that had ensued, the governor struck her and pinned her to the bed. The slave fought him off to free herself. As the struggle continued, she summoned a burst of energy to kick the governor in the groin. He yelled out a muted scream and slapped the slave across the face. She fell to the floor but tried to get up with the aim of attacking the approaching man. However, before she could make another move, he kicked her in the stomach sending her back to the floor writhing in pain. As she screamed, he dragged her out of the bedroom by her leg and into an adjoining room. Nana Yaa laid on the floor screaming in pain for a few minutes before one of the servants helped her into the room she shared with the other slaves.

The room turned dark as the servant retrieved the lamp after dumping her on the floor. The pain in her stomach was sharp and radiated through her entire body with every breath she took. Trying not to scream because of the pain, she sobbed and swore to revenge her humiliation. As she slipped into sleep, she realised how powerless she was as a slave despite the fact that she was a princess. She once again began to rationalise her ordeal. She reasoned that the darkness would at least help cover up her humiliation and pain, and blur the impact of her near conquest by the white man. She dropped down to the floor like a piece of worn-out rag, shut her eyes and cried herself to sleep.

* * *

"Maa I am thirsty."

"What?" asked a startled Jackie.

"I scared you, Maa?"

"No. Just a minute, honey," she said as she searched her daughters face and thought about the strange dream she had just had. She walked back into the governor's kitchen and took pictures of the place she had seen in her dream a few seconds ago.

"Are you all right, Maa?"

"Yes, I am."

"Were you dreaming?"

"I don't know, my dear."

"You had a strange look on your face, Maa."

"Actually, I may have day dreamed."

"I am thirsty," repeated Ama without paying much attention to what her mother said.

Mae heard Ama's question and turned to see what was going on. Jackie looked all right to her so she suggested, "Okay, let's go to the Elmina Hotel for some drinks. I think I've seen enough of this place for today."

"I've seen enough too."

Mae wrapped her arm around Jackie's shoulder and with the children flanking them, they started their descent from the governor's quarters.

"I agree. But we've got to come back and see the fort at a later date."

"Certainly; but we are coming back this evening to see the ceremony Franco talked about, remember?" asked Mae.

"How can I forget?"

"I don't want us to miss any of the festivities. After all, no one knows when we will come this way again."

"This is the dancing of the fetish people at the shrine of the god?"

"Yes."

"Franco said he's going to meet us this evening."

"I know that."

"Well then let's have early dinner at the hotel," suggested Mae.

"That's fine with me," Jackie said.

"That way we only have to go home and change to come back."

"That's right."

CHAPTER 5

"*O*kay, you promised to tell us an Ananse story today."

"You don't forget anything do you?" asked Mae looking through the driving mirror to Ama.

"You'll be finished by the time we get to Elmina."

"All right I will tell you my favourite Kweku Ananse story."

"What? Kekooo? What name is that?" asked Bianca.

"I said Kweku."

"Say that again," Ama pleaded.

"Say it with me, Kkkwwweeeku."

The children followed her lead and tried in various ways to pronounce the name.

"The full name of Ananse is Kweku Ananse, because he was born on a Wednesday," Mae said.

"I knew that. I have a friend in Baltimore, Kweku, and he explained that to me," said Jackie.

Mae exited from the western entrance of the university on to the highway and headed west toward Elmina. The evening sun had turned into a bright orange celestial object beckoning the travellers heading west to follow it to its destination. The orange colour seemed to turn red as they got closer to Elmina. Soon darkness would be taking over. The full moon was still a couple of hours away but the sun could not wait. Its destination beckoned it as Elmina also beckoned the travellers heading west. As strange as the colour of the sun looked the minds of the children were focused on the Ananse story Mae was about to tell.

"Does anyone know how Ananse became the hero of Ghanaian folk tales?"

"I don't think so," responded Ama.

"I'll tell you."

"We're ready."

"Once upon a time, there were no Ananse stories, and all the folk tales and stories had only one hero. Does anyone know who the hero was?"

"I don't think so," replied Ama again.

"Well, the hero of all folk tales was God. He solved all the mysteries and problems of world with his divine wisdom. He saved the poor and killed all the wicked people, dragons and the devils. He was the smartest and of course, the hero of everyone. One day, Ananse decided that it was time for him to become the hero of all folk tales. He felt that God lived too far away from us to continue to be the hero of our folk tales. So he decided to travel to heaven to ask God for His permission to replace him as the hero of folk tales. He made the long journey to heaven and the trip took him a couple of weeks. Mind you, he travelled on foot through rain, the hot sun, snow, ice and all the terrible weather conditions you can imagine. When he got to the gates of God's kingdom, he could not believe the sizes of everything. He looked like a peanut. Well, after explaining himself to the guards at the gate and going through several gates and corridors, he finally entered a room, the size of a football field. The room was beautifully decorated and there were angels all over the place playing horns and singing. Ananse walked slowly to the middle of the room where God's throne stood. Facing the huge throne, Ananse looked like a pinhead. But he was a determined man who was convinced that the time had come for him to be the hero of folk tales. He couldn't really look up to the throne because the light emitting from the throne was too strong for his eyes. He thought that because of his size he had to shout so that God could hear him. He had forgotten that God could even hear the quietest sound if there is anything like a quite sound. Well, he mustered enough courage to scream on top of his voice to briefly tell God what he had come to see Him about.

'Kweku Ananse, you didn't have to shout. I can even hear you think,' the room resonated.

'Oh my,' Ananse started to speak.

'Listen gentleman, I like your courage and determination,' boomed the powerful voice of God from the strong light that exploded with softness and serenity from the throne. 'But before I let you become the folk hero, I will put you to a test.'

Ananse's heart began to thump heavily but he maintained his composure and said under his breath, 'God, I am ready for the test.'

'All right Ananse, look down at your feet. You will find one grain of corn.'

Ananse looked down and saw this perfectly shaped grain.

'Pick it up,' God's voice boomed again.

Ananse did so, still keeping his head down and away from the powerful light that seemed to resonate with God's voice.

'Take the corn with you back to earth and in return, I want you to bring back to me one thousand men. I want one thousand strong men. And when you have accomplished this test, you will replace me as the folk hero of all mankind.'

'Huh?' asked Ananse.

Ananse stood there rooted to the ground and wondering what to say next, but nothing came to mind. He thought for a moment and realised the gravity of the problem. Finally, he protested but God insisted that if he wanted to be the folk hero, he had to pass the test. And with that, Kweku Ananse bowed and left for earth mumbling to himself in protest. When he arrived at the first town on earth, he was very tired, dirty and hungry so he went to the only motel in the town which was owned by the richest man in town.

'Ananse, you look very tired. Where have you been?' the rich man asked him.

'I am coming back from seeing God.'

'You are coming back from where?'

'From God. In fact, I am so tired that I can't talk much. All I need is some water for a bath and some sleep.'

'That shouldn't be difficult to provide.'

'By the way, I have in my possession a grain of corn that belongs to God so I want you to keep it for me. Please keep it in a safe place because I don't want to lose it and upset God.'

'Oh I will take good care of it,' replied the man.

The owner of the motel put the corn on his table with the aim of putting it in his safe when he was ready to go to sleep. But before he realised what was happening, his prized rooster had eaten the corn. The man became upset and afraid, not knowing how he was going to explain it to Ananse. He summoned some courage and woke up Ananse to tell him what had happened. Ananse became terribly upset and asked the man to give him the rooster so he could give it to God for replacement. The man readily agreed. So Ananse left with the rooster the following morning.

When Ananse arrived at the next town, he gave the rooster to his host for safekeeping and told him to whom the rooster belonged. The host promised to leave the rooster in the pen of his Guinness Book of Records award-winning ram.

'My prized ram is in the paddock grazing and I don't expect it to stay in the pen tonight so I'll leave the rooster in the pen.'

'That's fine,' replied Ananse.

Unfortunately for the host, the ram and many other sheep in the herd, stampeded into the pen that night killing the rooster.

Ananse was terribly upset once again and demanded to have the ram for replacement for God. The host did not argue about his request and Ananse left the following morning with the ram.

All this time, Ananse had still not figured out how he was going to get the thousand men. He pulled his ram reluctantly along, thinking and wondering how he was going to find a solution to this task until he reached the outskirts of the next town. He was so thirsty and hungry that he decided to stop at a farm to ask for water and find a good space for the ram to graze. The owner of the farm welcomed him, gave him food and water and asked Ananse to rest before continuing his journey. Ananse protested that he had an assignment to complete for God, and that he had to go. The farmer insisted that Ananse rest, so he agreed and decided to sleep for a while. Before going to sleep, he told the farmer that the ram belonged to God and that the farmer should take good care of it while he slept. The farmer put the ram in the corral for his cows.

While Ananse was sleeping there were violent thunderstorms and that caused all the cattle that were grazing in the fields to run back into the corral. The lightning and thunder frightened the animals into a stampede which resulted in the ram's death when the cows trampled on him. Ananse could not believe the bad luck that had followed him since getting the corn from God. He wondered what else was in store for him, now that the ram was dead. As he had done in the past, he asked the farmer for one of his cows for replacement. He was determined not to offend God so he insisted on taking one of the cows and the farmer agreed.

Entering the next major town before his hometown, Ananse saw about seven people on the way to the cemetery to bury someone. As soon as he saw the dead body a light went up in his head, and he began to smile. He begged the mourners to exchange the dead body for his cow. He stressed the wisdom in his proposal that the dead body was worthless to them and as poor as they were they could sell the cow for lots of money and he would take care of the dead body for them. It didn't make sense to the mourners but Ananse persisted to convince them. After a brief meeting between the mourners who were indeed very poor, they agreed to Ananse's offer. Ananse put the body on a cart, covered it with a white cloth and wheeled it into the town. He went straight to the king's palace and told him where he had come from.

'You have come a long way Ananse,' said the king.

'It's been a very long journey, and I can't even begin to tell you about my experiences.'

'Ananse, you look very tired, so let's talk later,' said the king.

'Thank you. Oh, by the way I am travelling with the grandson of God who is sleeping and I need a nice room for him,' Ananse requested.

'Certainly, I don't want any harm to come to God's grandson,' said the king who readily provided a room for the sleeping grandson of God which was actually, the dead body.

Ananse carried the body into the room and laid it on the bed. He then went back to the king and said 'I don't feel comfortable leaving him in there without any guards.'

'Indeed, I think we need some guards for God's grandson. How many men do you need?' asked the King.

'I think a thousand will be sufficient.'

'A thousand?'

'Yes, a thousand will make me comfortable, because of my experiences.'

The king quickly ordered a thousand men to guard the body.

Very early in the morning before the rooster crowed, Ananse was the first to slip into the room where God's grandson was supposedly sleeping. Quickly, he slaughtered a chicken he had stolen and spilled the animal's blood over the body. He then hid the dead chicken and came out screaming and crying that someone had murdered God's grandson. As anyone could imagine, there was confusion and chaos in the town. The king was very angry at his guards and very disturbed at the death of God's grandson in his palace. He summoned his elders into the palace to determine what could be done to appease God. After several hours of meeting, they could not come up with any solution. Meanwhile, Ananse was weeping uncontrollably and refusing to eat because he was mourning and wondering how he would explain such a calamity to God. While sitting under a tree crying, a messenger accompanied by ten soldiers from the king approached him. As soon as he saw the messengers, his heart skipped a beat.

'Ananse, you are wanted at the throne.'

Ananse's heart started palpitating fearing that he had been found out. He followed the messenger with the soldiers close behind to the King.

'Ananse,' the king called him.

'Yes, your honour.'

'What has happened here is very serious. I have investigated the murder and discussed all the issues with my elders and have come to the conclusion that you should help us find a way to appease God.'

Ananse could not believe his luck. His plan was about to work. He pretended to be in deep thought for a while and then started his speech. After a long speech about the responsibility of men to take good care of precious and irreplaceable things entrusted them, he cried sadly until many of the King's elders also started to cry. He then went into a long speech about fairness, punishment and the power of God whose grandson, he kept stressing, has been murdered. He concluded by saying, 'My king, I cannot think of a better way to appease God than this.'

'What is it, Ananse?' demanded the impatient king who had been groping for a solution.

'Since I directly hold the guards who were supposed to protect the grandson of God responsible for his death, I believe that sending them to God will be the best solution.'

'What?' screamed the head of the guards.

'You heard what I said,' Ananse replied.

'Wisely spoken Ananse,' said the king who readily agreed to Ananse's suggestion.

As far as the king was concerned, getting rid of the problem by sending the useless guards to God will relieve him of the problem of directly confronting God to explain himself.

'Ananse, I cannot thank you enough for your suggestion. You indeed are a very wise man as I have always thought. I will arrange to have all the guards ready and equipped for the long trip to God as soon as possible.'

Weeks later, and to the surprise of God, Ananse entered heaven leading a thousand men through the gates. God praised him for his wisdom and gave him his wish."

"So is that how Ananse became the hero of Ghanaian folk tales?" asked Bianca.

"Yes, that's exactly right. That's how Ananse became the folk hero of Ghanaian folk tales," responded Mae as she pulled into a parking spot near the Dutch Cemetery deep in the town of Elmina.

"The ride seemed rather short with your story, Mae," said Jackie.

"That was a good story," Bianca and Ama said in unison.

"Well, if you behave yourselves this evening, I'll tell you another one on our way back home."

"We will behave," Ama said.

"We promise," said Bianca also.

By the time they reached Elmina, the huge orange ball of the setting sun had disappeared and darkness had begun to envelope the town. The streets were filled with many people, most of whom were heading in one direction. The streetlights had been turned on but shadows had not been clearly formed.

Jackie's feelings and impressions about Elmina had, however, been formed. She had developed a strong bond and a sense of belonging to the town, especially the castle. Since their visit to the castle, she had been thinking about her dream. She wondered if she really lived the life of an Asante princess in a previous lifetime or it was her imagination running wild. Her feelings about the whole dream were too real and the memories were too vivid for her to dismiss the experience. She made a mental commitment to visit the slave quarters again, take pictures and videotape the place for safekeeping.

Throughout the journey to Elmina that evening, Jackie was unusually quite. It wasn't because of the Ananse story Mae was telling even though she found the story very interesting. She was subconsciously searching for answers to the deep feelings and sentimental attachment she had suddenly developed for this ancient town of early civilisation and slavery.

Getting out of the car, Jackie felt at peace with herself and could not wait for the ceremony to start. The anxiety in her voice was very clear when she said, "I hope Franco will be ready when we get there."

"Maa, you can't wait to get there, right?"

"Yeah, I think it's going to be fun."

"Yeah, I hope you are not going to dance like you did at that wedding in Accra. That was embarrassing," said Bianca.

"No, this is nothing like that," responded Mae, and added, "I don't think we will be allowed to even get that close. I understand that only the fetish priests and priestesses are allowed to dance in front of the shrine."

"Who are the priests and whatever?" asked Ama.

"Priests and priestesses," repeated Mae.

"The female priests are called priestesses, and they will be chanting and dancing to the god of the river all night."

"All night?" Ama asked.

"No not really. We just want to see parts of the ceremony, and we are not going to stay all night," said Mae.

The walk to where they were supposed to meet Franco was short. Just before they turned the corner to his grandmother's house, Franco appeared.

"You are right on time," he said.

They said hellos to each other and started to head in the direction of where everyone was headed.

"You don't want to miss anything, right? Actually you came at the right time. We don't want the place to be crowded or else we won't find a place to put our feet let alone sit."

"I'm anxious. By the way, thanks for taking the time to come with us so you could explain everything to us," said Jackie.

"Don't mention it. Let's keep walking to the shrine."

"What shrine?" asked Jackie.

"That's where the god of the Benya River is, and where the ceremony will take place," Franco answered looking at the perplexed Jackie.

"Did you say the god of the Benya River?" asked Ama.

"Yes."

"Is it scary?"

"Probably."

"No he's kidding. Right Maa?"

"No I'm not," said Franco.

"Come on girls, he's kidding. We won't see the god," said Mae with a chuckle.

"No, you're not going to see any god. You'll see the huge hut or the shrine of course, but the door of the shrine will be covered with a white cloth and only the fetish priests can go in there."

"You ain't kidding?" asked Jackie.

"Not really."

"So can we go in there?"

"No, no, no, no," he answered laughing.

"Why not?" Ama asked.

"You are not a fetish priest. Are you? Maybe only the

god's princess may be allowed in there."

"Does he have children?"

"I don't know them and I wouldn't know if I saw them," he said jokingly.

"What?"

"Are you serious that we can't go in there?"

"No you can't. What will you do in there?"

"I don't know."

"Jackie, you don't even know what the god looks like," said Mae.

"Okay Franco, educate us," Jackie interjected.

"I don't know what the god looks like either, but believe me it's not like a living being sitting there and ordering people around."

"So what does it look like?" asked Bianca.

Franco burst out laughing and answered, "I don't know. All I know is that it's a powerful spirit with supernatural powers to do many things that you and I can't do."

"Like what?" asked Bianca again with a sneer.

"Girl, you will not understand this. You are a bit too young to understand this. I'll try to explain it to you later. Okay," Mae said.

"Okay."

"Mae, I'll try and explain it to the girls and, hopefully make some sense out of the whole thing, if I can. I sometimes don't understand many of the things myself, but I'll try," said Franco as they approached the shrine with a host of other spectators.

Crowd had started gathering at the hut. Several wooden stools painted white had been set up directly in front of the shrine which was built with bamboo, straw and thatch. The stools are for the fetish priests and priestesses who were all clothed in white outfits and pacing back and forth, and sometimes disappeared behind the hut. There was a bigger chair in the middle of the white stools which Franco explained as belonging to the chief priest of the Benya god who is called Benya Komfo. The state drummers had arranged their drums in front of benches to the northern section of the hut, and directly opposite them were chairs for the Omanhene or the king of Elmina, chiefs and other important elders of the area. There was a big area in front of the white stools that was cleanly swept and well lit. It was obvious that the area would be the centre of the activities. Franco secured a favourable spot for his guests atop a five-foot pile of neatly arranged cement blocks directly across the hut, and with a clear view of the entrance. He sent someone to get cushions from his grandmother's house, which they used to make their seats on the blocks comfortable.

"I think we have a very good spot up here," remarked Franco as they settled into their seats.

"I thought I heard that this ceremony is a whole month thing. Is that right?" asked Jackie.

"No, it's actually six weeks."

"Six weeks?"

"Yes, but many of the things are not done on a grand scale like this or like the festival tomorrow."

"Okay, tell us about it," Mae said.

Ama put her head on her mother's lap and Bianca did the same to Mae as they waited for the ceremony to start. Franco sat between Jackie and Mae.

"As I said this whole ceremony is a six-week thing."

"We heard that already," Jackie joked.

"For the entire six weeks, there is a ban on fishing in the lagoon or the river and the sale of fresh fish and newly harvested foods like corn and yams is forbidden."

"Why?"

"I don't know for sure, but I think the purpose is to usher in the New Year after the ceremony with newly harvested crops and a bumper harvest of fish."

"I bet you can eat these fresh harvests in your house though," Mae said.

"Oh yes. It just doesn't have to be in public. As for fishing in the lagoon, there is a complete ban, and you better not get caught fishing. The other things that are prohibited during the six-week period include drumming and public dancing. The dead are supposed to be buried quickly and quietly, and mourning publicly is only allowed for a very brief period."

"That must be hard for many families, knowing how lavishly some of these funerals are done," Mae said.

"That's why some families keep their dead for weeks and bury them after the festival."

"You keep bodies that long?" asked the surprised Jackie.

"Sure. Bodies have been kept for months to build new houses before being buried."

"No, you're kidding!"

"Jackie, that's true," remarked Mae. "Depending on your status in society and how lavishly the family wants to make the funeral, the body could be kept for several weeks to complete all necessary arrangements."

"Yes, that's true, but as Mae said, it usually happens in the rich families."

"Is your family rich?" asked Ama.

Franco laughed and said, "Not as rich as I'd like."

"Anyway," continued Franco, "do you see the white flag and the woven cap on top of the shrine?"

"Yes, what is it?"

"That's a new cap up there. The old one is removed and thrown into the sea. All I know is that it is done in the first week and it's usually not a big ceremony."

"So the flag will fly for the whole year?" asked Jackie.

"Supposedly."

"Why?" asked Ama, but Franco ignored the question.

"During the second week, the young men make a huge fire near the river, sing songs and chase the women around with pieces of burning wood."

"You mean harass the women?" Jackie asked.

"Well, not quite like that. It's fun, especially with the kinds of risqué and funny songs they sing. The women also get their chance after the Bakatue Festival when they chase the men around with canes and flog them."

"Git out a'here. Do they really go around beating the men?" wondered Jackie.

"Some women do."

"That must be fun," Ama said.

"But why?" asked Bianca.

"The purpose is to get the lazy men off their butts to produce more food and bring in more fish from the sea. It's called sosoogya."

"What? So soldier?" asked the witty Jackie.

"That's funny. It's sosoogya," repeated Franco and continued, "I believe that one of the Asafo groups come over here to slaughter a sheep in preparation of bringing the Benya god here for the festival."

"What?" asked Mae in surprise, "from where?"

"A group of men paddle in a canoe at midnight to where the river originates. That's way up there in the thickets to invoke the god's spirit into the shrine," said Franco as he pointed west into the darkness.

100

"Wait a minute", said Jackie, "You mean they go to the god's place at midnight to what?"

"To perform certain ceremonies, drum and invoke the spirit to come into this shrine for the ceremonies."

"And how do they know the spirit is here?"

"Oh, you'll see what I am talking about when the drumming and dancing begin."

"You mean it's in there?" Ama asked pointing to the shrine.

"The god is there with others."

"Other gods?"

"Yes, other spirits."

"This is amazing," Mae whispered.

"Actually, this the third and final evening of this ceremony. I don't know if I told you its name."

"I don't believe you did," Mae said.

"It's called Dombo."

Mae and Jackie repeated it with different accents with the girls actually saying 'Dumbo'.

"I am not talking about the Disney elephant."

"No, no, no you didn't say it right," Mae chimed in.

"Hah?", asked Jackie.

"Let's try it again, Dombo."

This time the children also pronounced the word and they sounded better.

"That sounds better. In fact, when most people say the word, the b is silent. It sounds more like 'Domo'."

"I like that better; 'Domo'," repeated Jackie.

At that time Mae drew their attention to a retinue of men clad in white robes leading a group of chiefs and elderly men to the shrine, "Look at that."

"Here comes the Omanhene, the chiefs and the elders of Elmina."

"What's the Oma what?" asked Ama.

"The Omanhene is the king of Elmina," explained Mae.

"Which one is he?"

"That man right behind the child carrying the stool," explained Franco.

"Is it about to start?"

"It's about time," Bianca responded.

"Yes they'll be starting soon, now that the chiefs are here," said Franco. "They will pray to the gods, drum and dance 'til tomorrow morning."

Franco looked down at Ama and asked, "Can you stay up 'til tomorrow morning?"

"Yes, I can. Right Maa?"

Jackie looked at her and smiled, saying, "We'll see if you can."

"Well this ceremony is for all the seventy-seven gods of Elmina."

"Seventy-seven of them?" asked Jackie.

"Yes, seventy-seven."

"Holy mackerel," Jackie whispered.

"Seventy-seven of them and Benya is the head, or elder god, I believe."

"You mean all the gods are coming here?" again, Jackie asked.

"I wouldn't be surprised if they are here already."

"No wonder this place is crowded. There is traffic jam here."

"All of them in that thing over there?" asked Ama pointing to the shrine.

"They are spirits so they could even be sitting here with us listening to you," said Mae.

"I'm scared, Ma."

"They won't harm you if even they were here," Mae assured Ama.

"Yeah, right."

"They only harm the wicked and dangerous people, or those who have committed serious offenses and gotten away with them," explained Franco.

"And you are not one of them", said Jackie to her daughter.

"I am his princess," said Ama.

"I don't know about that."

"Okay."

"Franco, you didn't do any funky stuff during the year to bring them over here, did you?"

"I don't know, maybe I did."

"What do you mean? They are going to lay it on you tonight."

"I'm ready for them," joked Franco.

As the drummers assembled and the chief priest took the centre stage, Franco explained that certain important issues and disputes are often discussed and also settled here by the gods.

"It is believed that the gods possess the chief priest or any of the priests and priestesses and ask them to dance and communicate their commands to the gathering. The names of certain people who have committed serious crimes or immoral acts are mentioned in public and they are asked to pacify those they harmed."

"Is that really true?" asked Jackie.

"I don't know, but I don't doubt the powers of these gods."

"This is incredible."

"Yes, they are supernatural spirits created by God, and they have powers to do many things," said Mae.

"It's very powerful and deep. This is when there are also

all kinds of interpretations of actions by dancing priests and gossips of all kinds," said Franco with a laugh.

"Why are you laughing?" asked Jackie.

Mae who knew about such things explained, "the gossips are usually about who slept with whose wife and all those juicy gossips. Right?"

"That's exactly right, and many people are here to listen to those stories and about who is a witch and a host of other scandalous stuff."

"Maa I think they are about to start the Domo."

"Yes, Pumpkin."

"It's about time," said Bianca again.

Silence rippled through the area as the fetish priests and priestesses gathered in front of the shrine and began to take their seats. The men wore white cloth over their left shoulders exposing the right shoulders but leaving the cloth covering their entire bodies except parts of their legs and arms. The women wore two pieces of the white cloth, with the top half covering their upper bodies above the breasts. Their faces were painted with white clay and they all held small pieces of broom-like objects and walked bare feet. The chief priest stood up and waited for complete silence. The drummers and singers were all seated and ready. The chiefs and their elders were also seated with anticipatory glances at the chief priest. As silence began to envelope the whole area, Benya Komfo raised his hands and all the priests and priestesses got up from their chairs like infantry men obeying the orders of their commander. Benya Komfo opened a bottle of schnapps liquor, and began to pour libation. Pointing his head to the sky, he called God's name and thanked him. He proceeded to mention a litany of names beginning with Nana Benya, the chief god and went on to pour the libation.

Trying not to call any attention to herself even from those sitting near her, Jackie whispered into the ears of Franco asking, "What's he saying?"

"He is praying to the Benya god and calling the names of all the seventy-seven gods of the area."

"What? All of 'em?"

"Yep, all seventy-seven."

"Wow. We'll be here all night."

"Yep," said Franco with a chuckle, and added, "I'll tell you more about the gods later."

With another fetish priest standing behind him and shouting what appeared to be words of encouragement and support to Benya Komfo's incantations and libation, the ritual went on for about ten minutes. He continuously poured some of the liquor on the ground as he spoke. Finally, he doused the floor with lots of the drink before taking a sip of it from a tiny glass. Soon after pouring the libation, he entered the hut followed by two other priests to continue the ritual. While doing their thing in the hut, a loud scream was heard from one of the fetish priestesses who went into violent convulsions and started to mutter some words as her colleagues tried to restrain her. She bounced up and down the ground like a tennis ball, her movements becoming more and more erratic. With her colleagues still holding her, one of the drummers began to play the smallest of the drums in a steady rhythm. There was still silence from the huge crowd that had gathered in anticipation of what was going to happen next.

The drummer continued with the steady rhythm of the small drum held in between his legs as the priestess was being attended to by her colleagues. The atmosphere seemed uncertain and tense as the chief priest appeared to stay in the shrine for an unusually long time. The steady rhythm of the small drum continued to be the only sound disturbing the still air that had also enveloped the silent night. Jackie was anticipatory and so were the children and Mae who started having concerns about the safety of the priestess having convulsions. After what appeared to be a wait of eternity, the chief priest emerged from the shrine. No sooner had he appeared than the biggest drum in the group of the drummers begins to pound a heavy beat. With the lead of the biggest drum, the other drummers and percussionists eased themselves into the rhythm, and in no time they were all playing together in a steady rhythm. The beat moved faster and louder and as it reached a crescendo, the chief priest stood up and bowed before the chiefs who were seated opposite the drummers. He started dancing in circles and shaking the small broom-like object in his hands. He kicked the dust under his bare feet as he moved methodically toward the drummers and singers who were singing a beautiful melody. He danced for about three minutes before taking a seat. Meanwhile the priestess whom Franco later explained to Jackie and Mae to be possessed by one of the gods, had been carried off to the back of the shrine.

"This is truly amazing and interesting," said Mae holding on tightly to her tense niece and asking, "are you okay?"

"I am enjoying every bit of this," she answered.

As the ceremony went on, Ama relaxed on her mother's chest.

"Maa, your heart is beating heavily. Are you all right?" asked Ama of her mother who had remained very quiet.

Jackie did not respond to her daughter's question but no one paid attention to what the little girl said. She still sat quietly with her eyes glued to the fetish priestess who was dancing in a frenzied manner to the same heavy drumming and assorted percussions. She shuffled her feet in complex movements and swung her arms to the beat of the heavy drum and kept up a constant yell to the beat. With all eyes focused on her, a young woman who appeared to be in her late twenties and sitting close to the drummers suddenly fell forward toward the dancing priestess. In a flash, she removed the cloth which she had meticulously tied around her head and started speaking rapidly in the local language. The drummers kept playing as if nothing had happened. The priestess kept up her spirited dance and the crowd, knowing what was happening remained at ease. The young woman moved erratically as she kept talking and rolling on the ground. With some of the priests and priestesses trying to restrain her, she removed her blouse exposing her breasts. She appeared to have a sudden burst of energy and surged toward the centre of the circle, causing another priest to join the party trying to restrain her. She managed to free herself for a brief moment, danced erratically for a few seconds before she was brought under control and carried away to an area behind the shrine.

"She must be one of the god's princesses," Bianca whispered.

Jackie's heart continued to thump heavily. Franco looked at her and wondered what she was thinking about. Before he could ask if she was all right, Mae asked Franco, "Was that woman possessed?"

"Yes, and by the time we leave here, we would have seen a few others."

"What was she saying, anyway?"

"I couldn't understand a thing. It didn't sound like Fante

to me. I guess only the gods and those who speak their language know what she was saying."

"Are you serious?"

"Mae, I don't know. I am only guessing, because who else can understand all what she was saying. When people become possessed and start speaking strangely, the fetish priests are known to interpret what they say. In fact, I have a cousin who became possessed several years ago and started to speak one of the Ghanaian languages that she knew nothing about."

"Really?"

"Yeah. It was strange and it made a believer out of me. Evidently, there are some powers that can do such things."

"I know about the power of the gods and other deities, but I have not actually studied them in detail."

"Your friend, the Bishop of Kumasi is known to be an excellent source of information on minor deities. He'll be the best person to talk to. You'll learn a lot from him about the gods in Ghana."

"Yes I know that. I expect him in town next week."

As the conversation between Mae and Franco went on, Jackie still remained in deep reverie. Her daughter quietly wondered what was going on as she felt the heart beat of her mother thumping very hard. She removed her head from her mother's chest looked into her eyes for a few seconds and before she put her head back down, asked, "Are you okay, Mom?"

"Yes," she responded without any emotion.

Jackie still remained quiet with her eyes keenly focused on the entrance of the shrine. The drumming had become heavier with two priests dancing in unison. Mae realised that Jackie was either in deep thought or transfixed by what was going on with the dancing priests. Out of concern for the discomfort he suspected Jackie could be experiencing, Franco nervously put his arms around her. He wondered what Jackie was thinking with his arms around her but he ignored his thoughts and held her anyway. He realised that Jackie was trembling. He looked keenly at her and held her tightly hoping that the trembling would stop. However, it became a steady roll and continued at a slightly rapid pace.

Franco became alarmed and tried to draw Mae's attention to what was happening. As soon as he tapped Mae on the shoulder Jackie jerked forward and screamed causing Franco to quickly remove his arm. She yelled out a loud noise, and this time in Fante, drawing the attention of the spectators in the vicinity. Jackie fell headlong from the cement blocks throwing her daughter off her and hitting her head on the foot of woman standing next to them. The foot of the woman may have saved her from a possible head injury. Appearing not to have felt the impact of the fall, she yelled out again causing several people in the vicinity to scramble from the area.

Mae and Franco jumped from their seats to help her up, but Jackie went into a frenzy pushing the two of them away with a force that sent Mae reeling backwards and Franco backing away. Within seconds, she was jerking, dancing and moving toward the shrine. As the children shouted and cried at what they were experiencing, the heavy beat of the drums drowned the cries. Mae tried again to restrain Jackie from going to the fetish priest who was approaching her, but the crowd sealed her off. Realising that Jackie had been possessed by probably Benya, the god of the river, Franco maintained his distance and did not try to rescue her from the fetish priest who by then was helping Jackie to stay on her feet. Ama and Bianca started to cry not quite knowing what was going on, and wondering if they were losing Jackie. Franco held on to them assuring them that Jackie would be all right. Mae tried to muscle her way into the circle of the fetish priests and priestesses who were holding on to Jackie but she was held back by the crowd who knew that she could not do anything but just had to wait.

Jackie wrestled herself free from the two men holding her, and went into a frenzied incoherent dance to the heavy rhythm of the drummers. Circling with her arms spread out like a soaring eagle and muttering what sounded like the Fante language, she darted toward the door of the shrine. As she was about to touch the white cloth covering the door, she was restrained by two priests. Her neatly done hair had become dishevelled within that short period. With her arms stretched out and elbows locked as the priests held her, she stiffened her body, suspended herself in the air and kicked the air to the rhythm of the drums. Still muttering sounds in Fante, one of the fetish priestesses smeared her face with white clay and doused her with a liquid from a pot sitting near the entrance of the shrine. As the ceremonial rites were going on, the first woman who had been possessed by one of the gods recovered and emerged from behind the hut. The woman looked drained but coherent. She was helped out by one of the priestesses and within moments melted into the crowd and headed home to recover from her experience.

Jackie stayed in that tight position still kicking her legs, jerking her head and by this time, speaking Fante fluently. One of the priestesses listened intently to what she was saying. She repeatedly nodded her head in agreement to what Jackie was saying and spoke back, but Jackie seemed to be in a different zone. She was obviously not hearing what the priestess was saying. The priestess went into conference with the chief priest, Benya Komfo, and as she explained what was going on, Jackie suddenly lost the rigid structure she had maintained for the past minute or so, and suddenly became limp. She slumped to the floor face down dragging one of the priests holding her to the ground. The priest quickly got up and with the help one of his colleagues, carried the unconscious Jackie to an area behind the shrine.

"Jackie is possessed by Benya," said Franco and he tried to assure the children that she will recover soon and be released.

"Will she be alright?" Ama inquired.

"Yes. She's indeed the god's daughter now."

"You don't mean that."

"No, not really. Just kidding."

The festivities continued with the spiritually possessed chief priest dancing and talking to the chiefs and the elders. The chief priest became possessed by several gods in succession and kept dancing for several minutes. During all this time, Jackie was in a house behind the shrine, and the activities continued without a pause.

CHAPTER 6

"Shu's wakin up, shu's wakin up," shouted Daisy Rae to the children.

"Mama, mama."

"Jackie, Jackie."

"Mama, you alrah?", asked her daughter.

"Shu's gwine be good."

"Mama, you alrah?"

"Call Susta Mae, call Susta," Daisy ordered.

Ama and Bianca darted across the grounds and path that separated the slave quarters from their master's mansion. Standing in the kitchen in her white apron, Mae looked out the window and saw the children running toward the house. She hurriedly dropped the pot she was holding, and fearing the worst, dashed out to meet them.

"Lawd Jesus, wha wron' chillun, wha' wron?" she inquired.

The children responded in unison "shu's wakin up, shu's wakin up."

"Lawd hab merci on the chil. Lawd hab merci," said Mae as she continued her fast trot toward the slave quarters.

She entered the room where Jackie had been laying for the past hour and saw her sitting on the floor with her head on Daisy Rae's chest.

"Shu's alrah, shu's alrah Susta."

Mae knelt down beside the two of them and with the children looking on, she held Jackie. Tears welled up in her eyes as she wondered what could be happening to the lady. She started to pray silently as she always did before going to sleep and after waking. She then kissed Jackie on the forehead and asked.

"Chil wha' hapun. Wan sometin to drink?"

Jackie nodded her head in the affirmative, upon which Ama got a cup of water sitting on a table and gave it to Mae. With Mae's guidance, Jackie drank the water.

"Lawd, thank yew, Oh! Lawd thank yew," Mae kept saying as she held the drained woman in her arms. She could see fear and uncertainty in Jackie's eyes.

"Wha' wron' Jackie? Wha' wron'?" Mae asked in a whisper.

"Nuffin. Nuffin wron.'"

"Is it wha' happun on de farm tiday."

"I don' kno.'"

"Shuah?"

"I jes don' kno.'"

"Youah brada is gwine be alrah." She assured her that her brother would be okay.

"Alrah, Mae, Alrah."

"He's gwine be fine."

"Alrah."

Mae believed that the rumour on the farm about Jackie's brother, Spike, and the thought about her horrible experience when she became pregnant with her daughter, Ama, may have frightened her to faint. She was aware that Jackie could not survive on the plantation without her brother and the fear of what could happen to him caused Jackie a lot of anxiety. Jackie was concerned that Spike would be sold off and lost forever. Mae spent some time with Jackie to calm her down and assured her that the chances of Spike being sold were remote. After all, she, Jackie, was the favourite person of the slave master's favourite daughter. But deep within Mae's heart, she felt that there was something else wrong with Jackie. For over eight years, Mae had tried to find out what really troubled Jackie and why she sometimes recoiled into a shell but try as she did, Jackie never opened up.

"I don' truss no white fokes," Jackie said

"Don' say dat."

"I don' Mae, I don'."

"No, no, no Jackie."

"One day you'll see fo youasef."

"I kno', bot don' say dat."

"Alrah."

Mae did not want the conversation about the distrust they had for white people to continue, especially in the presence of the children, so she stood up. She had always maintained that even though they all distrusted their master, the children should at least be taught not to hate but to be cautious of people. Jackie's distrust of their master was no different from her own distrust, but Mae was very silent about it. Being the most trusted slave on the plantation, Mae could not afford to let her deeper feelings be known. She did what was expected of her to earn the trust and the confidence of her master. In her opinion, that was the only way she could help her fellow slaves and her family. After all she had managed to keep all of them together through her influence, and that was why she was still confident that Spike will not be sold.

When Mae and her sister emerged from the room, there were a few other slaves standing outside the door waiting to hear about the condition of the plantation's favourite singer in the slave quarters. There had been so much anxiety since Jackie fell hard and lost consciousness earlier on in the afternoon.

The late summer evening was cooler than the slaves had expected, but nothing was going to stop them from their evening entertainment. The weekly ritual of storytelling and singing of songs from their motherland by this second generation of slaves who trace their roots to the Gold Coast was the most anticipated event on the farm for all the slaves. Thus, unless it was raining, the show was bound to go on. Luckily, the temperature was in the mid sixties, and that was considered cold.

The owner of the plantation and the slaves, Mr. Jack Silverman, had recognised the importance of the Friday evening gatherings of the slaves and had made efforts to accommodate them. As was usually the case, Mr. Silverman had asked for work on the farms to stop early that Friday afternoon and that was about six o'clock instead of the usual time past sunset.

Jack Silverman was a successful farmer with over one hundred acres of tobacco and cotton farms. Believed to be one of the wealthiest men in the south, he was also considered to be the state's most influential voice in Washington even though he was not a politician. A tall man standing six feet five inches and weighing a little less than one hundred and ninety pounds, he appeared lanky but had a very deep voice that boomed through the walls of his mansion when he became upset. Mr. Silverman was even more known for his baritone voice than his wealth because he did not flaunt it. His taste in clothes and his wife's taste in jewellery were legendry and a clear indication of their wealth and class.

Being one of the most powerful businessmen in North Carolina, Jack Silverman was considered a chief maker in the politics of the state. Most of the politicians in the state owed allegiance to him because of his wealth and the power he wielded throughout the state and in Washington. He was the financial backbone of some of the legislators, and the Washington establishment knew and respected his power.

At about 8:30 in the evening, as three male slaves prepared wood to set the bonfire for the evening storytelling, Jackie, Bianca and Ama sat on a bench and watched. As usual, Jackie had composed a song for the evening's gathering. She had managed to convince Mae and Daisy Rae that she felt fine after sleeping for over an hour. Daisy Rae fixed her dinner, rubbed her down and saw her off as she left with Ama and Bianca for the 'Tree Bottuum', the gathering place of the slaves for entertainment. The meeting and entertainment site of the slaves was under a huge spruce tree, which the slaves literally referred to as "a meeting at the bottom of the tree," thus the name, 'Tree Bottuum'.

Sandwiched in between the children on the bench and cuddling them, Jackie began to sing a song she had composed for the upcoming wedding of Catherine Silverman, the only daughter of Jack and Stella Silverman.

"My susta is marry
Lor' sho dem de laat
In de mornin and in de ebnin
Lor' sho dem de laat
We gwin t' pray fo you
Lor'sho dem de laat
A'am huppy
Shu's huppy
He's huppy

We's huppy
Lor' sho dem de laat
Lor' sho dem de laat.
Aam huppy
Mis Catren is huppy
Massuh Anteny is huppy
We's all huppy"

Jackie sang her composition two times with the girls listening intently. After the second time, the children joined in the chorus, and soon the three men who had been arranging wood for the evening fire also joined in the chorus and clapped their hands. The six of them stood in the middle of the arranged benches and continued singing the chorus, clapping hands and stumping their feet.

The approaching horses pulling the carriage of Senator William Smith caused them to stop singing. The horses pulled in front of the bedroom mansion of the Silvermans. The driver of the carriage opened the door for the Smiths and Mr. & Mrs. Silverman emerged from the imposing house followed by Catherine.

The Silverman mansion is an exquisitely clean and an imposing colonial building painted in white with black trimmed windows. Thanks to the numerous slaves who worked tirelessly to maintain the grounds of the three-year old mansion in an impeccable condition. Even though he was a farmer, Mr. Silverman helped design his two-story building and supervised its construction. His wife Stella was a perfectionist with a sophisticated taste, and she chose the Victorian furniture and the fixtures for the house. She even commissioned an artist in Washington DC to make individual portraits of her family when the house was completed. The stairs leading to the upper floors of the house were lined with expensive paintings purchased at auctions in Washington DC, and all the rooms in the house also had at least two beautiful oil paintings. Mrs. Silverman was an avid collector of art, a habit she developed from her father, a wealthy farmer from Georgia.

The baritone voice of Mr. Silverman that greeted the senator and his wife also announced the presence of their son, Anthony who was engaged to be married to Catherine Silverman. They exchanged greetings, with Anthony kissing the hand of Catherine and her mother.

The Smiths were frequent visitors to the mansion and all the slaves on the farm knew who the bald, pot-bellied man was. Mr. Smith was a staunch conservative whose sole purpose in Washington appeared to be fighting for slave and state rights, and representing the interests of Mr. Silverman. Unlike his friend Mr. Silverman, the senator was not very sophisticated or as rich. He was an eloquent speaker though, loud and witty. He was rumoured to have slept with some of his slaves several years ago, causing his first wife to divorce him. Despite his shortcomings, Mr. Smith was a trusted friend of the Silverman family and with the backing of Jack, he was elected a senator.

Looking at the Silvermans and the Smiths from a distance, Jackie felt a terrible chill. The thought of her family being separated if Spike was sold raced through her head also. She was aware of the rumour that some slaves were going to be sold and that Mr. Smith might even buy a couple of them. The thought about the events of the day sent shivers through her. She froze in place for a brief moment and before the children and the three men could find out what was going on with her, she sat on the floor and asked for water to drink. She still felt weak and faint so the men helped her to her feet and took her home.

Turning to look at slaves who were gathered at 'Tree Bottuum', Catherine Silverman saw the other slaves help Jackie to the slave quarters. From where they stood about three hundred feet from the house, Catherine could not clearly determine what had happened because it was dusk. Jackie was the specially assigned maid of Catherine and they had developed a close friendship over the years. Catherine tried to get the attention of her parents as her friend was being taken away, but before she could say a word, Anthony Smith, her fiancé, pulled her into the house closely following their parents. Catherine sensed that something had gone wrong but she did not pursue her instincts because her lover did not even give her the chance to think about Jackie. She felt guilty, but also felt helpless at that time.

As she followed Anthony into the house, she thought and wondered why ever since she introduced Jackie to her fiancé, she had never heard him say any complimentary things about her. Catherine found it strange. In her opinion, Jackie was the most likable person she had ever met. Besides, she had become a close friend and a reliable maid. A woman with whom she had been associated for almost eight years. She had even decided to ask Jackie to live with them as their chief maid when she married Anthony because of her dedication and her trust for her. But despite all the good things she said about Jackie, Anthony never said anything favourable about her.

"Maybe, the story about his father sleeping with slaves may still be unsettling to him that's why he doesn't care about these people," Catherine continued thinking as they entered the dimly lit living room.

Jack Silverman and the senator excused themselves from their wives and went into the study room. Catherine and her fiancé sneaked up into her bedroom while their mothers stayed in the living room. As Mae prepared to serve the Silvermans and their guests coffee and freshly baked cookies, Ama and Bianca ran into the kitchen and waited to tell her what had happened to Jackie.

Mae run back to the slave quarters worried about what was wrong with her friend this time. Mae was of the opinion that fear and extreme anxiety about the future of her brother and her family must be causing that. Additionally, knowing what Jackie went through when she gave birth to Ama, Mae was determined to protect and prevent any harm from coming to the woman. However, what continued to puzzle Mae was that Jackie usually felt fine after about an hour's sleep and showed no effects from her experience.

Bursting into the room she shared with her sister, Jackie and the children, Mae felt Jackie's head to see if she had a fever. She knelt down beside the sleeping woman and wondered for a moment about what could be wrong with Jackie. She looked helplessly in the eyes of Daisy Rae and stood up.

"Daisy I thunk shu's resing' now," said Mae as she stood over Jackie.

"Wha' hapun?"

"I doan no," replied Daisy, "she jus fall don, and dem chillun and dem brung her."

"Lawd hab merci on har."

"Susta, I thunk she hab to sleep. Shu'll be alrah."

"Yeb, shu'll be alrah," repeated Mae. Wha' I doan understan is whar she fain' all da tam."

"I doan kno."

"I doan kno' masef. Am gwine tell Mis Catren," said Mae

as she left to go back to the mansion.

"Wha you gwine to tell Mis Catren?"

"Abat Jackie."

"No. Don' tell her yit."

"Why?"

"B'cos Jackie doan trus dem peple."

"Wha'?" asked the infuriated Mae.

"Yeb you hea me."

"Wach youah mouf, Daisy. Mis Catren been good to eberybody. She been good to Jackie. She love Jackie and shu's gwine to hep har. All dem yeas we been heah, Mis Catren hep Jackie mo' dan anybode. So wha' you say dat."

"B'cos she doan truss dem white fokes and you kno' dat."

Mae seemed to understand what her sister was saying, but she felt that the issue was irrelevant at that time. She was concerned more about the health of Jackie at that moment and did not think that the issue about whether Jackie trusted white people was relevant. Nevertheless, she made her point clear to her sister that despite their feelings about all the white people, Catherine had never given them any reason to feel that way. Besides, they needed to make the best out of the situation in which they found themselves and try to help the ailing woman. Deep down in Mae's heart she wanted the white people to pay dearly for what happened to Jackie several years ago when she became pregnant with Ama. Her strong conviction that the white man was responsible for her agony was somewhat proven, but no one was held responsible. She wanted someone to pay for that dearly. But whom? She did not know. However, she was convinced that someone would, one day. That was also a key ingredient of her daily prayer which she had a strong conviction that God listened. She was indeed convinced that God will answer her prayer.

*   *   *

Darkness had completely descended on the slave quarters. Senator Smith and his son, Anthony, had finished their visit and left. Before leaving for the slave quarters that evening, Mae had also said her usual "Gud naat Mam, Gud naat Catren, and Gud nat Massuh." Except for Mr. Silverman who nodded in response, the others had responded, "Good night Mae."

Unlike the Silverman's mansion that was usually quiet in the evenings, the slave quarters was alive. Tonight, as was the case on most Friday nights 'Tree Bottuum' was literally on fire. The fire built by the slaves was huge and bright, and the shadows of the slaves danced to the tunes of the flames. The flaming tongues of the fire constantly broke free and vanished in the darkness repeatedly reminding some of the slaves of what freedom could taste like in the north. Nevertheless, none of them seemed to be thinking about escaping that evening. If even anyone was planning an escape, it did not show on their faces on that Friday evening. Only the excitement of the evening and the yellow flickering flames illuminated their faces.

When they were all seated, the eldest slave, Uncle Josef, as they all called him, said a short prayer for the family members who had died and those whose whereabouts were not known. He always made mention of the peace and freedom those who had died were enjoying and asked for God's guidance for those who had been sold and those who may have been caught trying to escape. Uncle Josef had always counselled against escapes. He was of the opinion that life on the plantation was not great, but since no one has ever come back to tell them about the good life of the escaped slaves, he only relied on the pain and agony captured slaves endured as the basis for his counselling. He believed that slaves captured in their attempts to escape were suffering and needed God's strength to endure the pain of their capture. So he prayed for them. After his short prayer, Jackie's voice pierced the stillness of the night with the favourite song of the slaves.

"I am tar, Hep me Lawd,
I am lonle, Hep me Lawd,
In ma sleep, Hep me Lawd,
Glorey to de Lawd
Glorey to de Lawd
Eberyday,"

As soon as Jackie completed the one verse song, the whole group burst into the song with rhythmic clapping of hands and stamping of feet.

"I am tar, Hep me Lawd'
I am lonle, Hep me Lawd'
In my sleep Hep me Lawd,
Glorey to de Lawd'
Glorey to de Lawd'
Eberyday,"
Glorey to de Lawd'
Glorey to de Lawd'
Glorey to de Lawd'
Eberyday.
Glorey to de Lawd'
Glorey to de Lawd'
Glorey to de Lawd'
Eberyday."

As the volume of the song began to rise, most of the slaves stood up, stumping their feet, clapping their hands, dancing around the fire and singing harder. The singing went on in a controlled frenzy for a period of time before they settled into melodic humming of the song, and then faded out as all heads turned in the direction of Mae.

Mae beamed a huge smile at being the centre of attraction and with a voice of authority yelled out, "Midi, midi, midi, midi, midi."

"Yo," responded the slaves to Mae's utterances in unison.

"Midi, midi, midi, midi, midi," repeated Mae.

"Yo."

Midi, midi, midi, midi, midi."

"Yo."

"I am gon' finsh de storey dat I didn' finish las' tam wen de rain com fallin' don.'"

"Oh yea. Oh yea. Gud. Alrah," and other words of approval echoed through the gathering in excitement.

"As I was tell'n youah all, las tam, ma grea' granfada was a chief in ma billage. Ma granmada was a princes' and was butiful lede. I doan foget har face yit. Dat butiful face, ma Lawd," Mae said with a broad smile that showed her pride and admiration for her grandmother.

There were whispers of appreciation of Mae's grandmother's beauty from the gathering and she acknowledged them with nod of her head.

"O Lawd, shu's a butiful M'aam," echoed one of the elderly men in the group.

"One day we is tol' dat som wite folks gwine t' fight us an' teke ouah lan' an' gol'. Ma granfada haf mo' gol' dan de Lawd gib one man. Ma gramada tol' me abat a room in de groun wher nobodi an' nuffin can go in der ecep' ma granfada an' harsef an' one ole man."

"Youah grafada rich, Mae?" asked one of the slaves.

"Yeb, we's rich somtam ago. We was, somday," said Daisy to the laughter of the group as she insinuated that the slaves were rich sometime ago in the Gold Coast.

"Yeb, but we rich no mo," responded Mae, drawing the attention of the slaves to reality with her comment, and drawing more laughter.

"Yeb we no rich naw. We doan hab nuffin, nuffin, nuffin," said the eldest man in the group, Uncle Josef. "We git de Lawd, dat all we hab. Gowon Mae," he ordered.

"Yeb as I wa' sayin', onle a few peple kno' whar all dem gol' an' trasure was hid. An' it was imposibl' no matta how good anybode sarch to look fo' dem gol'. Wel', dis ole man was ma granfada bes frien',an' he rich too. Dat niggah kno' eberytin' in dat hawse. He eat in da hawse, drink in da hawse an' Lawd kno' always wid ma grafada an' he waef."

"Wha, dem coun' de gold?" Spike joked.

"You funny. One day, de ole man git los' from de village. Dem village peples sarch eberywhar but dey no fin' 'im. Afta two days sombode say de gods mus' hab kill 'im. Wen ther's gwine t' be war de village gib de sprit of sombode to dem gods. So eberybodi say dat de ol' man bin kill by de gods so dat we gon win de war."

Mae paused for a short moment for the story to sink in. She had always been puzzled by the idea of sacrificing people to the gods before wars. She knew that the gods did not take the people by themselves and it was fellow human beings that sacrificed their kind for the safety of villages and those going to the wars.

Believing that an important elder of the village had been sacrificed by the village for the impending war, no other sacrifice was made. In preparation for the attack, advanced scouts were dispatched to assess the strength of the enemy and their positions. Upon returning, elaborate plans and traps were laid by the surrounding villages for the enemy. Two days passed and there was no attack. The plan of the villages was never to attack but to lay in wait and lure the enemy into their traps. Most of their wars had been won with strategic plans of trapping their enemies and weakening them with their defensive strategies before finally attacking to destroy everyone in sight. They were known for their discipline, bravery and savagery. As a result, the enemy soldiers always feared to attack. For their defence, the white men and other armies relied on local inhabitants as spies and paid them well with gold.

The intensity on the faces of the slaves clearly showed as Mae advanced her story. Waiting for Mae to describe the triumph of his ancestors over the white men, there was the anticipation of a detailed description of how the enemy soldiers were slaughtered in the war by these savage warriors. Being a gifted storyteller and knowing how to capture the attention of her audience, Mae played along and built the suspense of the outcome of the war. She had the undivided attention of the slaves whose faces were brightly lit with the flames from the fire.

She described in detail the dangerous trip by a second advance group to determine why the attack by the enemies had not materialised.

"Wen dem peple com' back dey tel' de chief dat dem white sojahs was packin' dem guns an' thins t' go back. So ouah sojahs den com' home."

She paused again and asked, "D'you rember dat ole man dem gods kill fo' de village?"

"Yeb, ya, yup, yap...." the gathered slaves responded.

"Dat ole niggah run 'way to spy fo' dem white sojahs. He tol' em 'bout all de plan of his peple an' mo'. He kno 'bout eberythin' an' how de peple wil' fight. So he tol' dem white soljahs to make as if dem gwine back so 'is peple wil' not be rede to fight. Den de white soljahs go arawn' an' attack ouah villages from de back. Dey kill many peple in de village an' teke de res slabes. De ole man hep dem white fokes steal all de gol' an' trusha in de village. Dey kill my granfada and his waef. Dey kill all de ole fokes in de village an' as I say agin, took eberybody as slaves. Dat whar I'm hea t'day."

"So wha' happun to de ole man?" someone asked.

"Dem white fokes gib 'im gol an' took 'im to de coas'. My mama tol' me dat dem Fantes kill 'im wen dey hea de story, and took all 'is gol."

The loud applause at the end was not because of the good story that had captivated their imagination but the death of the old man who betrayed his people. The slaves had developed a sharp sense of loyalty to each other and were sensitive to distrust. As the applause roared through the gathering it started to take on a rhythm. Soon, they were stamping their feet, dancing and singing again.

"Go tell it on the montin
Ober the hills and ebrywhere
Go tell it on the montin
And lit my peple go
Lit my peple go
Lit go, lit go
Lit my peple go
Lit go, lit go
Lit go home to Gol Cose
Lit go home to Eas Cose

Lit go home to Wes Cose
Lit my peple go
Lit go home to Gol Cose
Lit go home to Nor Cose
lit go home to Sar Cose

The story telling and singing continued for about two more hours with two of the elderly men telling Ananse stories and other stories about their origins in the Gold Coast and how their fathers survived the long and difficult trips over the oceans to America. Just like the war stories that Mae was used to telling, the slaves loved to hear about the experiences of their grandparents and especially, stories about their people who managed to run away from their masters and secured their freedom in the north. The elders were very good at telling these stories and knew how to captivate the attention of the audience, so they made up some of the escape stories, many of which occurred on previous plantations they worked before coming to the Silverman plantation. Obviously, there were no witnesses to corroborate their stories and the escapees never came back to tell their stories so they had the leeway to develop and fill the stories with lots of suspense, and that was what the slaves loved most.

As was usually the case after every gathering at the "Tree Bottuum", Jackie led them in the good night song. With smiling faces on most nights, but with heavy hearts on some occasions, depending on the last story told, the slaves sang the usual good night song as they dispersed to go to their shacks.

"Oh my Gawd,
Le' timoro com'
We gwine home
Le' timoro com'

Take me to ma home
Le' timoro com'
Le' tit com'
Le' tit com'
Le' tit com'"

"Oh my Gawd,
Le' timoro com'
I am tar'
Le' timoro com'
Guar' me thru' the nat
Le' timoro com
Le' tit com'
Le' tit com'
Le' tit com'"

"Thank yew my Gawd
Le' timoro com'
Gib me my stren'
Le' timoro com'
To do my wok
Le' timoro com'
Le' tit com'
Le' tit com'
Le' tit com'."
"An I hope to gain de premis' lan',
        Glory, Alleluya!

CHAPTER 7

$\mathcal{H}$ours before the rooster crowed, many of the slaves lay awake in their beds waiting for the first light. Unbeknown to each other, Spike and his roommate, John, were also wide-awake. Staring in the darkness and wondering what tomorrow had in store, they independently thought about the new man who had terrorised them on the plantations during the past week. They searched their minds, searched their souls and looked for solutions in the dark, but found none. Work had never been so hard and the days on the farms had never been so long. Separately, all the slaves wondered when the terror, tension and the difficult working atmosphere on the farms would ease or cease. The night and the peace they seemed to enjoy would not last forever. Unfortunately, they were painfully aware of the approaching first light and what the day had in store for them.

"Why was the old supervisor let go?" They often wondered but deep down their hearts, they knew the reason. Obviously, they enjoyed the relatively relaxed working conditions with him. Working conditions they terribly miss now. Being a slave and working twelve to fourteen hours a day in the scorching sun of the summer was extremely difficult in the first place, and a wicked slave driver was what the slaves did not need.

Concerned that production on the farm had not met his expectations on two consecutive seasons, Jack Silverman hired the best farmhand in the county for his farm. Jack had the resources to hire the best farmers and slave drivers. He also had funds to buy the strongest slaves to give him the best harvests every season. Thus, the mediocre harvests of the past two seasons that were far below his expectations caused him to look for the best man for the job. Two weeks ago, he hired George Williams to be in charge of his farms.

George was a legendary man in the county. He was known to do wonders with slaves on cotton and tobacco plantations. Standing about five feet ten inches and weighing about 130 pounds, he was lean and mean, and that reputation also made him famous in the county. He wore a goatee and a thick red moustache that eclipsed his lips and matched the colour of his hair. Whenever the lips parted on rare occasions, they showed teeth badly discoloured from years of chewing tobacco. George had become the symbol of the devil on the Silverman plantation, and within three days of his arrival the slaves named him Devil George. All the slaves had reasons to think about Devil George every morning before work began on the farms. Not only because he had instilled fear in them, but most importantly, because he had become the master's enforcer and all the slaves knew that when Devil George spoke, Jack Silverman listened. Even Mae had reason to fear Devil George for the simple reason that he was on the plantation for the sole purpose of making money for his master, and no one except maybe his daughter Catherine stood in the way of the powerful Silverman and money.

Ever since arriving on the farm, Devil George who had been around slaves on various plantations for all his adult life realised that Spike was not a hard worker, but the clown of the farm. He hated slaves whom he considered lazy. And, as he had done on other plantations, had used the lazy slaves as examples to instill fear into the others by remolding them into some of the best workers. His philosophy was that, his boss paid lots of money for the slaves so he had to get the best out of them. Besides, he was aware that he could not own slaves, but he could use them and his skills as a farmer to make money for himself. As a result, George made a personal commitment to change the working habits of Spike a few days after his arrival on the plantation.

Spike was the most jovial slave on the farm. He was known for his sense of humour, his never-ending funny jokes about the white man and even some of his fellow slaves. Spike sought the attention of fellow slaves with his jokes. Devil George, on the other hand sought the attention of his slaves with his authority. George liked being in charge and hated being interrupted or distracted when he was addressing his slaves. A week after his arrival on the plantation, Spike mimicked the expressions of Devil George who had the habit of spitting and stabbing his fore finger at the slaves as he spoke, his unusually red eyes wide open and popping out of their sockets. The muted laughter that Spike's joke drew caused Devil George to ask the slaves in his southern drawl, "whaar's de matter? Am ah funne?"

No one answered. The silence of the slaves caused Devil George to come down from a small platform he was standing on to address the slaves. He moved slowly and menacingly forward to the nearest slave and with his red eyes about to pop from their sockets, asked again, "whaar you laughing?"

Still no one answered as he moved past the first slave who happened to be a very frightened woman who was literally

132

shaking. He looked into the woman's eyes bringing his nose close to hers for a moment before pulling away. He made a quick turn to his left and pointing to the face of a man standing behind the woman, he slowly asked in the deepest southern drawl,

"Aa said, whaar you laughing, boy?"

"I doan laf massuh," responded the slave.

"Agaiiin I ask. Whaar you laughing, boy?"

"Massuh...I...?

"Shut up," he screamed and moved on to Daisy Rae.

"Whaar's funny?" he screamed.

"Massuh, I doan kno."

"What you say?" still screaming.

"I doan kno' suh."

"Whaat?"

"Ples, massuh I doan kno."

"Ha, haaaaa, haaaa..." he laughed annoyingly.

"Massuh.."

"All rah, if you won' tell me whaa's funny, then I'm goin' faan out maself."

He then cursed under his breath, "Aaam teach them niggahs who ar am."

Devil George gravitated toward Spike. With brown spittle from the huge tobacco he was chewing on dripping from the corners of his mouth, the slaves sensed that there was going to be terror on the farm that day. The slaves knew that he was very angry. They also sensed how much he disliked Spike.

Devil George stood in front of the shorter Spike, and towering over him, asked, "whaar was funny, boy?"

"I doan kno," suh."

"Then whaa do you laugh?"

"Massuh, I doan laf, suh."

"I saw you laughing, niggah boy," he lied with his mouth in Spike's face.

"No suh," he said in a pleading voice as he tried not to aggravate the situation by removing his face from the heavy tobacco breath of Devil George.

"Alrah boy, come wid me."

"Yeb, massuh."

"I'll teach you niggahs not to fool wid me. You hear?"

"Yeah suh."

"I say, you hear me, boy?"

"Yeb massuh."

George led Spike to the edge of a huge plot of cotton field and placed a stake at the beginning of the plot.

"Follow me, boy," he ordered.

Without saying a word, Spike followed him through the mature cotton fields. Turning around to face the other slaves who were about a hundred yards away, he told Spike to harvest what he had marked for him before the end of the day. There were four hours left before the day ended and it was obvious that Spike would not be able to complete the work. Devil George was having the last laugh.

Walking back to the other slaves who were waiting for their group assignments, he reminded the slaves that no one was to say a word or make a sound when he was speaking to them. At the conclusion of George's lecture and assignments to the group supervisors, the slaves departed to work. As the slaves walked away from Devil George, they turned to look at Spike who was alone in a section of the cotton fields. He looked very tiny and pathetic by himself among the tall stalks of cotton plants. A sight that caused Devil George to start laughing to himself.

The end of the day did not bring any relief to Spike or any

of his concerned colleagues. He could not complete the work and no one, including Devil George was surprised. Leaving to go back to the slave quarters, Devil George called him by tapping on his shoulder.

"Boooy."

"Yeb suh."

"Did you finish the work?"

"No suh," replied Spike as he tried to avoid George's eyes.

"Tomorrow you start all over again," he said softly.

"Yeb suh," said Spike without understanding that he was starting the work from scratch.

"Alrah boy."

"Yeb suh."

"You go on home."

"Tank yew, suh."

The journey back to the slave quarters was filled with conversations about how wicked and terrible Devil George was. Daisy Rae thought about how she could get Mae to help ease the pain, but realised that her influence at the mansion did not extend to the farm. No one seemed to know what to do to help any of them or Spike who was in a far worse position than anyone of them. Unbeknown to Spike, a couple of the slaves devised a plan to help him when Devil George was attending to the tobacco farms. Spike, however, was humbled by the problem of dealing with Devil George who had clearly established his dislike for him. There was nothing Spike could do about his situation. He could only pray that the all-powerful George will have mercy on him. A fleeting thought of killing Devil George flashed through his head, but it quickly evaporated because, he could not even plan it let alone carry it out. Besides, George was stronger and more powerful for Spike to challenge in any form of combat. In the end he resigned himself to dealing with the situation to the best of his strength and ability. After all, he thought, that he could only do what he was capable of and nothing more or nothing less.

Devil George dominated his dreams and thoughts all night. He could not shake off the smell of his tobacco breath from his mind or the red hairy face that terrorised him that afternoon. Even though they were all concerned and feared Devil George, never had Spike felt so helpless since his arrival on the plantation.

After about an hour of tossing and turning in the wee hours of the morning, Spike felt that his roommate was also awake.

He asked, "John, you awoke?'

"Yeb," a voice in the darkness responded.

"I is awoke too."

"I kin git sleep, John."

"Me too."

"Wha we gwine do?"

"I doan kno."

"I'm fraid, John."

"Me too," said John to the surprise of Spike.

"Massuh, say eberybode is gwine farm today."

"I kno."

"Wha Debil George gwine do?"

"I doan kno."

"John, I kint harbes all de catton."

"I kno' dat."

"I kint do de wok eben in two days."

"We's fine way to hep you."

"Dat's gwine make treble for us."

"Whaaa."

"Debil George gon kill us."

"So wha' you gon do."

"I doan kno."

"You jes shet youah mouf timoro."

"Den wha?"

"We hep you, Spike we gon hep you."

"I afraid."

"No worry. We wait timoro."

"Okay, John."

"Jes go to sleep. T'is no mornin' yit."

"Yeb."

Spike did not want to talk anymore about tomorrow with John so he turned around to sleep. He had a lot of respect for John who was a few years older and well respected on the plantation. John was a cunning man who had made his intentions known that he could not stand any white man, not even Mr. Silverman. He was a big well-muscled man, standing six feet three inches and always gave the impression that he feared no one. He was rather quiet, hard working and full of action but with the temperament of a saint. As a result, Spike took him very seriously and listened to his advice. Spike realised that any form of help could only be received tomorrow and that indeed John may have some of the answers to his headaches. If anyone had the will and the means to help any slave through fair of foul means, it was John and most of the slaves were aware of his capabilities.

"I gwine try to sleep, John."

"Yeb. Timoro is gon com soon. Git sleep."

Jackie had heard about his brother's problems on the farm through Daisy Rae, and that worried her tremendously. Just like the other slaves on the plantation, she knew of the power of Devil George and was aware that to the extent that all his

137

activities on the farm were toward making money for Mr. Silverman, not even Catherine could intervene. Besides, Jackie was smart enough to realise that Spike's suffering was a minor issue on the farm and none of the Silvermans would really care about that. In fact, it was a non-event to the Silvermans and the white workers. Catherine would lend a sympathetic ear to Jackie and that would be the extent of her concern. She was also aware that the personal welfare of a slave working in the cotton or tobacco fields was not much of a concern to her father. Mr. Silverman was concerned about production and money, and not a lazy slave who is having problems on the farm. Jack Silverman would rather get rid of the slave and he had done so in the past.

Waking up in the morning, Jackie said a short prayer for her brother because she was painfully aware that if the situation worsened, the final and lethal blow would be Spike being sold and that would be devastating to her. That would mean death because it could also be the last time she would ever see her brother again. She had witnessed the pain one family on the plantation had endured a few years ago when their only son was sold off. In fact, that slave's mother still talked about her son and wondered if he was still in the county, state or escaped to the north or even still alive. It was a painful experience for all the slaves on the farm when the woman pleaded and wept bitterly as she ran after the cart taking her son away. The thought of losing her brother in a similar way sent shivers through Jackie. She felt helpless and could only pray and hope for the best.

"Gud mornin."

"Morney," responded Spike to Daisy Rae.

"Some butiful mornin', Spike."

"Yeb."

"You alrah?," she asked as she sat between Spike and John.

"Only de Lawd kin tell."

"I kno'. Only de Lawd kin hep us."

"Yeb, susta."

"So wha you gwine do?" she asked as the horse drawn cart carrying them and several other slaves to the farm pulled away. Two other carts filled with slaves followed as they made their way through the winding roads to the farm.

"We's gwine work dem catton bos ti def," Spike said with a smile that also drew a chuckle from Daisy Rae and John.

"You's funny, Spike."

"Wha kin man do?"

"Nuffin, but wha you kin do," answered John.

"Yeb, yeb, John. We only do wha we kin, and de gud Lawd do de res," said Daisy Rae as she tapped Spike on the shoulder.

"Yeb. But somtams, the Lawd tell we to do wha we tink is rah. He's gon do nuffin for us. We do wha we do ouasebs and den pray dat he forgif we if we don wron.'"

"I tink so. But de Lawd's gwine gaad you," said Daisy Rae wondering what exactly John meant.

"Yeb, sometam de Lawd no wan to kno wha' we's doin.'"

"Hmmm," Daisy Rae sighed and looked at Spike.

"Yeb, John is rah."

"Ahah?"

"Yeah."

"Yeb, I is rah. De Lawd wan man to protek 'imsef. Tis a sin wen we no protek ouahsefs and led de whiteman abus we. Uh ha, Gawd wont forgif we. We haf to protek ouahsefs. You hea? We haf to. You tink de Lawd's gwine smile on me if I no protek my brada Spike and led somtin hapun to he. Noooo, no. T'is no rah. T'is no rah," he said shaking his head.

"Susta, we haf to do wha we haf to do fo all dem niggahs

hea."

"Tank yew Lawd," Spike said realising that John will not let him drown.

"Oh yeb, tank de Lawd we hab men lak yew," repeated Daisy Rae.

"Lak me?" joked Spike.

"Aha," Daisy Rae responded.

The rest of the journey to the farm was made in silence. No one mentioned George's name. After all he was part of them and was just another face on the farm that they had to deal with, as painful as it was. The only difference is that he had the power. The power to unleash terror and fear. The kind of fear that shot through the heart of Spike as the cart came to a stop on the farm.

Devil George was usually the first on the farm and the last to leave. This morning was not different from any other. Holding a long stick and waiting at his usual platform next to one of the barns, his mouth was full of tobacco. He folded his arm and watched as the slaves assembled in front of him. He gave them brief instructions to continue with the harvesting as had been done the previous day. The early morning meetings were George's way of informing the slaves that he was in charge on the farm. Rarely did he change assignments in the mornings for any of the three groups of thirty slaves he supervised. When the slaves left the gathering, he motioned Spike to follow him back to the plot that he had earmarked for him to harvest the previous day.

"Boooy, you goin' finish this field tiday."

"Huh?"

"Booy, don't waste ma taam."

"Massuh, I kint finish harbes all dem catton."

"You whaa?"

"Ples massuh."

"Yeeb, you will."

"Massuh, I kint."

"Now lissen to me, booy. If you don't finish de work, I will see that you are sold. You hear?" threatened George with a smirk.

"Ples massuh."

"You hear boooy?" he snarled with emphasis.

"Yeb, I gon do ma bes."

"That's whar I wan ti hear, booy."

"Massuh, I gon tra."

"All raah, git to work."

"Yeb suh," Spike said knowing that he was fighting a lost battle. He knew that it was only a matter of time when Devil George will come back and make his life more miserable for not completing the work.

Devil George left Spike at the edge of the plot and turned around to see three slaves including Spike's roommate, John, looking at them. As soon as their eyes met, the slaves moved into a barn. He followed them to the barn, but before he entered, the men emerged with huge baskets and proceeded to join their groups in the cotton fields. He stared at them and did not say a word as the men dissolved into the fields.

Having worked for about six hours harvesting cotton, the supervisors who helped Devil George on the farm ordered the slaves back to the barn for a break. As was his usual practice also, Devil George visited the tobacco farms of the Silvermans, which were about a mile away. During the absence of Devil George, John and his two friends went over to help Spike harvest his assigned plot of cotton. Realising that they could only help Spike during the break when Devil George's assistants were not looking on, the three men and

Spike did not take any break, but worked like possessed men throughout the break which lasted about three quarters of an hour. The length of the breaks were determined at the discretion of Devil George or his assistants and they usually depended on weather conditions.

When the supervisors returned with the slaves to the fields, Spike was still harvesting cotton. It was evident that he had not taken any break. However, it was also evident that an incredible amount of the plot had been harvested and even the untrained eye could determine that Spike could not have done all that work by himself. As the slaves emerged from the barns and dragged themselves back to the fields, they mumbled their surprise among themselves. The supervisors looked on in awe but none of them made any comments. They marched the slaves back to the fields and went about their work as Spike continued his work.

No sooner had the slaves gone back to the fields than the horse-drawn cart carrying Devil George arrive on the farm. He jumped from the back of the cart, put on his dirty black hat and discharged a stream of black spit before proceeding to the barn. He was met at the gate by one of his supervisors. He had a brief discussion with the supervisor, which ended with the supervisor pointing in the direction of where Spike was working.

*   *   *

When Catherine pulled up in the cart in front of the mansion, Jackie was not there. The early September sun was still hot and everyone knew that Catherine could not take the heat of the sun. In her anxiety to have the cart readied for the afternoon ride she had forgotten to wear her hat.

142

Jackie emerged from the house with the yellow straw hat that Catherine usually wore on their afternoon trips to the farms.

"I see dat you not haf youah hat."

"I know I can always count on you."

"Hea, Miss Catren," Jackie said handing over the hat.

"Thank you."

"Dats alrah."

"All right let's go."

Just as Jackie was about to climb into the cart, Mae emerged from the house. She was followed by Mrs. Silverman who never liked the idea of the two girls riding around by themselves without an escort. She was not about to stop them because she had somehow gotten used to the two of them riding to the farm throughout the summer. Nevertheless, she always cautioned them to be careful.

Leaning on the frame of the door next to Mae, she cautioned again, "Be careful and don't be long."

"All right, Mama."

Jackie climbed next to her mistress and with a quick yank of the rope by Catherine the horse started a slow trot. Gradually, the horse picked up speed and with Mae and Mrs. Silverman looking on, the cart vanished from sight.

The first thing that came to Jackie's mind when they left the vicinity of the house was Catherine's wedding plans. She has been ecstatic since Catherine told her that her singing group would be allowed to entertain the guests at her wedding. Since Catherine's promise a couple of weeks ago, Jackie's group had practiced almost every evening when the slaves were not dead tired from the day's work on the plantations. Their best practice sessions were on Friday nights when all the slaves gathered at "Tree Bottuum" to entertain themselves and tell stories. Besides working on her song, Jackie had also engrossed herself with Catherine's plans for the wedding and their new home. Jackie was familiar with the Smith family and knew that even though the senator was not as particularly tidy as Jack Silverman, his son Anthony was a meticulous individual and Catherine was counting on her to help maintain the house. Even though the upkeep of their house after her marriage was Catherine's concern, that issue was not on Jackie's mind that afternoon. Her mind was on the wedding itself.

"So are you going to sing the song, Jackie?

"No, Miss Catren."

"I want to hear it if it's good."

"No. Youah Mama tole me to keep it serprise."

"It'll be a surprise?"

"Yeb."

"And my Mama knows about it?"

"Yeb, I sing fo her."

"No, you didn't."

"Yeb. She lak it."

"I don't like surprises."

"Yew gwine lak dis one," said Jackie with a giggle.

"I told you I don't like surprises. That's one of the reasons why I was upset with Anthony."

"Yew upse' wid Anteny?"

"Yes."

"Wha?"

"I wont tell you why."

"Please."

"At least not now."

"Alrah," conceded Jackie.

"So will you hum it for me?"

"Wha'?" asked Jackie not knowing what Catherine meant.

144

"Hmmm,hmmm,hmmmmm," Cathrine hummed.

"Oh, I hum fo you?"

"Yes."

"Alrah."

Jackie hummed the song for a brief moment and the melody sounded so good that it brought a smile to Catherine's face.

"I like it," said Catherine.

"Am glad yew lak it."

"I want you to sing it now."

"No, Miss Catren. No," protested Jackie with a laugh.

"All right, that's all right. I hope Anthony will love it. Actually I think he will. I like the song myself. At least what I heard sounded so good."

"Am glaad."

Because of the conversation about the wedding, Jackie had not thought about where they were going. Over the past few days, they had gone to the tobacco farm.

"We go to de catton farm?"

"Yes, Jackie, or do you have another place in mind?"

"No, Miss Catren."

"We've not gone there all week. I just want to see how far the harvesting has gone."

"Am shua massuh's gwine hab a good harbes' dis yeah."

"Well, I certainly hope so. George seems to be working hard and my father is very pleased with him."

"Dat man, Debil George?"

"Yes."

"Dem slaves no lak him."

"I know that."

"He no lak Spike at all."

"Why?"

"I doan kno."

"Why are you saying that? I have heard that he doesn't treat the slaves well, but I haven't heard anything about Spike."

"Well Catren, somtin hapun yesterday at de fam."

"What happened?"

Jackie finished telling Catherine the story of what had happened on the farm the previous day as they approached the farm. She was more concerned about the likelihood of her brother being sold than the work he had been asked to do by Devil George. The story Jackie told did not make any deep impression on Catherine nor did she show any concern because she strongly felt that Spike would not be sold by her father. He was a member of the big plantation family and unless he had committed a serious crime or tried to run away, he was not likely to be sold. At least that was her father's unwritten rule, and she knew that. Jackie was of a different opinion, because she had heard about the power of Devil George. As a result, her strategy was to counter the power of George with that of Catherine if the issue of her brother being sold ever came up in the house of the Silvermans.

"My God, what was that?" asked Catherine when she heard a loud scream from behind the first barn as they approached the farm.

"I thunk somebode is gettin' whuped."

"What?"

"Yeb. Somebode is gettin' whuped."

"Good Lawd, it sounds bad."

"Uh huh."

"My God, let's see what's going on."

"Alrah".

The two women jumped off the cart, and picking up their dresses to enhance their mobility, they hurriedly run to the

146

back of the barn. The scores of slaves looking on blocked the view of Catherine and Jackie as they approached, but the black hat of the man in the middle could clearly be seen. Seeing Catherine approach them, the slaves made room for her to pass. Jackie followed closely and the sight of her brother bleeding in the back from cuts caused by the force of the whip caused her knees to weaken.

Whether he saw the two women approaching or he simply did not care about Catherine's presence, Devil George kept his eyes focused on his target. He screamed at the top of his voice, "Who harvested the cotton?" with every stroke of the whip.

"Boy, I said who haarvested d'catton," he said, cracking the whip on the back of Spike.

With a very weak voice and in tremendous pain, Spike tried to speak but nothing came out of his lips. Jackie screamed at Devil George to stop but before she could finish her plea, Catherine jumped into the semi circle formed by the on-looking slaves and screamed at George to stop.

"Stand away, Miss Catherine."

"No you must stop now."

"Whaaat?"

"I said, stop."

"I'll not 'til he tells me who helped him harvest d'catton."

"Why?"

"Huh?"

"Look at him. He is fainting."

"He mest tell me now."

"I said, stop it," she screamed.

It had become clear there and then that they were both trying to establish their power and authority in the presence of the slaves, and while Catherine was more concerned about the fainting slave who was bleeding from his wounds, George was concerned about establishing that he was in charge on the farm. As the discussion continued, Catherine took a position between George and Spike and that may have influenced his decision to stop the whipping. He however, did not stop the screaming.

"Boooy, you mest tell me now or else you sleep here on de farm wid me."

"George, I am taking him back."

"Whaar?"

"Back to the slave quarters," Catherine said.

"Whaar?" asked George again.

"I'm taking him away."

"Aam sorry, Miss Catherine," said George as he took about three steps menacingly toward her.

"I am sorry too George."

"Boooy, I said you're staying here wid me."

"I don't think he is capable of speaking now. Just look at him. You can talk to him when he gets better," she seemed to plead.

"Let him tell me."

"I said he is not capable of it. John, untie him," she ordered.

"All raah, Miss Catherine," conceded George as John walked past them to untie Spike.

George discharged tobacco-laden spit and backed away as John untied his roommate. There was a collective sigh of relief from the slaves because if Catherine had not arrived, Spike would have been beaten to unconsciousness. Jackie sat on the ground and cried as Daisy Rae and two other female slaves comforted her. At the direction of Catherine, John was helped by the two men who assisted Spike with the harvest to carry the bloodied man to the back of Catherine's cart. Slowly the slaves departed from the scene of the punishment leaving Catherine and George alone still staring at each other. Jackie stayed on the ground watching the two powerful people on the plantation discuss what had gone on.

Catherine knew that she had interfered with George's work, but she felt strongly that her father would understand her reasons for doing so. She picked up her hat, which had fallen during her efforts to reach George, shook off the dust and put it back on her head. Turning to Jackie who was still sitting on the ground, she took a quick glance at her and walked past to the horse-drawn cart. She was very upset. She climbed into the cart and with Jackie sitting next to her brother, she commanded the horse to start their journey back home. The trip back was made in silence with each of the two women swimming in their own thoughts and Spike drowning in pain. Catherine thought about how she was going to convince her father that she had done the right thing while Jackie thought about the pain her brother must be experiencing and how soon he would heal. Catherine was aware of her father's unconditional love for her but she was not sure if her mother would side with her. She shrugged her shoulders and took comfort in the fact that her father's opinion was more important to her anyway.

CHAPTER 8

*I*n utter silence, Catherine sat at the dinner table hoping that her father would not say a word about the argument she had with her mother a couple of hours earlier. She was not even sure if her father had been told about the argument because she had gone to her room, and in her pain and disappointment that her mother could not see her point, had cried herself to sleep. She slept deeply for about an hour and did not even hear her father call when he entered the house from his trip to Charleston. Catherine was still upset at her mother because she not only felt that she was right, but that her mother was insensitive.

"Catherine. My dear Catherine, what is the matter?" her father asked as he sat down to dinner.

"I'm sure Mama has told you everything. Hasn't she?"

"No. Not quite."

"What hasn't she told you?"

"That's not my question."

"I don't want to create anymore problems."

"Oh no."

"Yes, Father."

"No one said that there is problem."

"Then, why does Mama look so upset."

"She's not."

"I am not upset, Catherine."

"You were an hour ago. What has changed?" Catherine asked.

"Listen Catherine," said Mr. Silverman, "I don't know what actually happened on the farm. I have only heard what your mother told me, and she may have a point."

"How can you say that?"

"All I'm..."

"How can you say that?" she repeated with disappointment, interrupting her father.

"All I am saying is you don't belong on the farm."

"I know that, Father."

"Yes."

"But that's not the issue."

"What is it then?"

"I didn't go to the farm to interrupt George's work. I didn't go there to create any problems. I only went there to see how the harvesting was going. Is there anything wrong with that?"

"No, but...," her father tried to speak.

"I know that I don't have any power on the farm."

"Right."

"That's right," Mrs. Silverman interjected.

"But I cannot stand by and see anyone beaten to death."

"Did you find out what happened?"

"I don't have to. Do I?"

"I think you should have."

"After the person is beaten to death?"

"Has any slave been beaten to death on this plantation before?"

"No, but this plantation has not seen George Williams before."

"Well?"

"That's a fact, Father."

"I still think you should have left them alone," said Mr. Silverman.

"I still think what I did was not wrong."

"But you interfered," said Mrs. Silverman.

"Yes, I did, and it was the proper thing to do, Mother."

"Maybe. Maybe not."

"Well, I saved a human being."

"It may have been proper, but try not to do that again," said Mr. Silverman trying not to offend any of the women.

"I'm sorry," Catherine said.

"That's all right," replied her father.

"But I think you need to talk to George."

"Let me worry about that."

"You need to do that, Father."

"I will talk to him."

"Maybe that will help all of us."

"I will do that, Catherine."

As Jack Silverman finished his sentence, Mae walked in with a pot of soup. She had been listening to the discussions of the Silvermans as she went about her business and walked in and out of the dining room. She knew that she could participate in the discussion but she deliberately kept her comments to herself. Earlier on when she went upstairs to wake Catherine up for dinner, Mae had assured her that she supported her action and that what she did at the farm was the right thing. Obviously, Mae did not take a position during the afternoon argument between Mrs. Silverman and her daughter for fear of offending Mrs. Silverman. Even though her comments were often tolerated in the house, Mae tried not to overstep her bounds especially when the parents were on the same side of an issue against their daughter, as it appeared to be with the incident on the farm. Mae was known not to mince her words, and even though Mrs. Silverman liked her frankness and honesty, there were times that she could not stand to hear her opinion, especially if it contradicted her position. Mae was aware of that, and realising that she had to spend most of her days with Mrs. Silverman, she developed a good sense for when to speak her mind and when to shut her mouth.

Walking back to the kitchen, Mr. Silverman asked her what she thought about the whole issue.

"Massuh, I doan thunk I kin do good work if you whup me all de tam. Whupping doan hep nobody. Especial if you whup de boy to collapse. It doan do nuffin fo nobody," she said confidently.

"So what, if the person was terribly wrong?" asked Mr. Silverman.

"I no say doan punish dem slaves who cause treble. Yeb, dey hab to be punish, but doan kill his soul. Gawd gib man one soul and no man hab to teke anoda man's soul. Onle de Lawd kin teke de soul," said Mae as she exited.

"She never ceases to amaze me with her words," Jack Silverman said with a smile.

"But she's right," Catherine said.

That's her opinion," said Mrs. Silverman.

"Well let's leave it alone."

"Good," Mrs. Silverman agreed.

"I'll handle it later with George."

Jack Silverman had seen slaves whipped before, but had not seen anyone whipped to unconsciousness. Deep down in his heart he knew that it was cruel to go to that extent and felt that her daughter may have done the right thing by stopping George. He knew about the cruel and tough nature of George but always recognised the wonderful work he has always done with slaves. However, he did not want to tell Catherine in the presence of his wife, that she was right. Besides, he also felt that saying that to the hearing of Mae could be embarrassing to his wife, so he reserved his judgment.

"Catherine. Dear Catherine, you still did not tell me what happened."

"I thought Mama told you."

"I don't think you even told her the whole story because you were upset when you came home. Right?"

"I think so, Father."

"Well then."

Leaning back on the chair, Catherine told her father what had happened on the farm over the past couple of days. Jackie had narrated the story briefly to her when she helped her take Spike to his room. After listening to Jackie's version of the story, which was indeed the truth, she went home hoping that her mother would see the wisdom in her decision. Unfortunately, her mother did not, and the ensuing argument between them in the kitchen caused Catherine to storm out of the kitchen in tears.

After listening to his daughter's story, Mr. Silverman folded his napkin and stood up from the table. He walked over to his wife, patted her on the shoulder and whispered for a few seconds into her ear. He moved over to his daughter, kissed her on the head and also whispered into her ear. They all cracked smiles on their faces to which Mr. Silverman acknowledged with his own dry smile.

*   *   *

It has been about three hours since he was helped into his room by Catherine and his sister. In Spike's estimation, he has never experienced such pain and anguish in his life. A life which by all indications appears to be entering a hazardous and an unpleasant phase under the supervision of Devil George. Jackie stayed with him and nursed his wounds from the whipping until he drifted into a short sleep that lasted about fifteen minutes. When he woke up, the pain that radiated through his body as he tried to get up caused tears to well up in his eyes.

"Tis alrah, Spike. Jes lay don."

"Dat man tra to kill me."

"I know."

"He tra to kill me."

"You be alrah."

"Doan foget to thunk Miss Catren fo me."

"Yeb. I do dat."

"I hurt bad."

"You be alrah."

"I hab ti be. I kint fight Debil George if I no stron.'"

"Spike, yew still funny. You gwine fight Debil George?"

"Yeb."

"Wid wha?"

"Wid ebery tin I hab."

"You beder shush youah mouf."

"My mouf's shush."

"Git some wata," she said as she picked his head up to drink.

"Tank yew, susta, tank yew."

"Dats alrah."

As always, the arrival of the horse-drawn carts was announced by two barking dogs. Shortly after the slaves jumped off the carts, Daisy Rae entered Spike's room followed by John and one of the slaves who helped Spike harvest the cotton.

"How's he?" Daisy Rae asked, thinking Spike was asleep.

"De Lawd no teke ma breth yit," answered Spike.

"No, de Lawd will protek you."

"De Lawd gib me stren' too becos no white folk's gon sass wid me," John said.

"Ah, ah, is niggahs who doan sass wid dem peple," said Jackie.

"Alrah, nobody's gon sass wid me. Dat Debil man's gon pay fo dis. I no see anybody whup lak dat. Neber, neber. Becos of catton?"

"Catton is money," Daisy Rae said.

"No meke no sense t'me. De man do de habest. Whar whup him if he finish de wok. Dats wha Massuh Siberman wan, rah? Fo de catton t' be habest. So if we don it, whar whup de boy. Meke no sense t' me," said John trying to find a sound reason for the cruel treatment.

"I tank Gawd dat Miss Catren come sabe us," said Daisy Rae.

"Yeb, I tol' Jackie to tank her fo me."

"Mae come hea' and she say Missus Siberman no lak wha Miss Catren do."

"Whaa?" asked Daisy Rae in surprise.

"She fuss wid Catren bad," Jackie continued.

"I no tink Massuh Siberman will fuss wid his dawta" said Daisy Rae.

"I kno dat. He lob dat girl too much."

"Mae say somtin to Missus Siberman?" Daisy Rae asked.

"She no say nuffin."

"I kno' why."

"Yeb, no wan git in treble."

"Oh yeb, but she's gwine talk what on her min' tonat," Jackie said.

"Oh, yeb de good Lawd kno' dat."

"Yeb wen de Massuh com 'ome."

"Dat wen her mouf will fla."

"Yeah, go susta."

The conversation in the room went on for a few more minutes before Daisy Rae and Jackie left. Spike had managed to get up with the help of John and was eating some soup. He ate in silence wondering how his friend John would help him this time. George was not just any white man John could confront or threaten. He was powerful and was their master on the plantation. Even though Mr. Silverman was the ultimate authority, George was responsible for the use of the slaves and Mr. Silverman listened to him. Spike knew that they were up against a formidable entity unlike the previous man who was responsible for the farms and did George's work, and whom John managed to threaten without any serious consequence. John was also aware that George was a different man and would not be easy to deal with. In fact, John had not even entertained any idea of exhibiting his influence and power among the slaves to George. However, what happened on the farm that afternoon gave him cause to be concerned about George. He had underestimated the wickedness of Devil George.

John sat silently across from Spike eating a bowl of rice and beans. He raised his head at Spike and with a nod of his head and a smile, assured Spike that everything will be all right. Spike knew John well enough to realise that he was not going to let him die at the hands of George. He also took comfort in the knowledge that he had a voice in the Silverman mansion that could say a word on his behalf.

Their dinner was interrupted when the barking of the dogs announced the approach of horses to the Silverman's mansion. John extended his body to look through the window to find out who was approaching and before he could focus his eyes on the horse, Spike said, "Dat's Debil George."

"I tink you's rah. Yeb tis him alrah."

"De Lawd's gwine kill 'im befo he kill me."

"No I'm gwine git him befo de good Lawd," whispered John.

"I sure hope so."

"De Lawd kno's I will."

"Huh?"

"Aha," John whispered.

Spike sensed the seriousness of John's utterance and pretended not to take him seriously. John also ignored Spike for a moment and continued with his dinner. When he finished his dinner about five minutes later, John left the room and disappeared under the cover of darkness into one of the rooms behind their shack. A few minutes later he re-entered the room.

Back in the Silverman mansion, George's arrival was announced by Mae who let him into the house. Catherine was standing on the elliptical stairway carved from mahogany when George entered the house. She gave him a cold stare, walked down the stairs past him and followed Mae into the kitchen as Mr. Silverman approached. George's eyes followed the two women and did not realise Mr. Silverman enter.

"Hello George."

"Mr. Silverman," he greeted.

"Come on in."

"Yes Sir," he said following Mr. Silverman into his office.

Mr. Silverman closed the door behind them.

George lived about a mile and half away from the Silverman's so responding to his boss's request to meet with him was not a problem. George was not Jack Silverman's friend and the business relationship that they had was based on Jack's trust for his farming and slave management skills.

As was usually the case, Mr. Silverman started their meeting with George's report on the tobacco farm. The discussion later turned to what has been Mr. Silverman's headache for the past two years, the cotton plantation. They discussed how the harvesting was progressing and the performance of the new cotton press for baling. No mention was made of the sale of any slaves or the purchase of any slaves either when it became clear that work was progressing smoothly on the farms and that they were going to have a good harvest. Mr. Silverman was even more impressed with the speed at which the work was progressing and seemed to have forgotten about the cause of the tension in his house that evening.

As the discussion about the farms ended, George began to anticipate a query about the afternoon's incident. However, Jack Silverman made a conscious decision not to ask George about the incident on the farm, feeling that it would not be appropriate to reprimand George for doing what he felt was best for the farm. After all, Jack Silverman was seeing significant progress with work on the farm and was pleased.

With the meeting over, the two men emerged from the study to see Catherine sitting in the living room by herself.

It was not clear if she was waiting to answer any questions her father had about the afternoon's incident. Nevertheless, she did not show any sign of disappointment as the men appeared to have finished whatever they met about without asking for her input. In her mind, she felt that she had made her point, and to the extent that her father had not made a big issue about the incident, she would do the same thing again if the same situation arose again.

Walking toward Catherine, George bowed politely and said, "Good evening Miss Catherine."

"Good evening," she responded without looking at him.

"I must apologise for this afternoon's misunderstanding," said George.

"I don't need any apologies."

"I'm still sorry."

"I think it's Spike who needs an apology."

"Miss, I don't apologise to slaves."

"I'm not surprised."

"He needed to be punished for lying."

"I thought you asked him to harvest cotton and he did it. Right?"

"No he didn't do it himself."

"But the cotton was harvested?"

"Yes. But..."

"But what? Isn't that what we all want?" Catherine interrupted.

"I believe so Miss Catherine, but if I don't maintain control on the farm, your father will lose money."

"Lose money for harvesting cotton?" she asked sarcastically.

"Not really."

"But what?"

"I believe that's true Catherine," said Mr. Silverman.

"Right?" she asked in surprise.

"There should be some discipline and control on the farms."

That comment by her father convinced Catherine that it was not necessary to continue with the conversation. After all, her father was agreeing with George.

Turning to her father, Catherine said, "Good night," and climbed the stairs.

"Good night Catherine," responded Mr. Silverman as he saw George to the door.

In his mind, George felt vindicated. He knew that Jack Silverman did not really care about who was whipped or who was asked to do what on the farms. What he cared about at the end of the season was how much money he made from his farms, and George was right in his assessment. Climbing onto his horse, he felt a sense of invincibility, because, he had just been given a vote of confidence by Mr. Silverman. He did not feel that he needed any boost from his boss, but his decision to ignore the disagreement he had with his daughter made George feel even better. There were many slaves on the plantation who on the other hand, did not feel good about what happened, and many of them wished they could have the opportunity to lay their hands on George. But who dared to confront George.

Chewing his tobacco and riding back home in the cool evening breeze, George thought that he saw someone cross his path about twenty yards ahead of him. It was dark, but the clear sky and the full moon that enhanced his visibility also created long ghostly shadows. Thinking that it may have been a person and likely to be a slave attempting to run away, he slowed down his horse to a slow trot. He focused his eyes on a couple of big chestnut trees that he thought the person could be hiding behind. But before he could get closer to the trees to see who or what was behind them, he felt the weight of a rock at the back of his head. The force of the rock and the sudden jerk and scream by George startled the horse. Sensing that they were in danger, the horse took off at a terrific speed and vanished from the sight of the attacker within seconds.

In his life, George has never been attacked by anyone. At least, to the best of his knowledge and certainly not in his adult life. He did not know whether it was the effect of fear or anger that caused him to start sweating as the horse approached his house at an unusual speed. The fast sprint of the horse at that time of the evening caused a few men to emerge from their homes. They watched George who was not known to ride that fast at that hour dismount and rush to his home with his hand on his head. Three of the men realised that there was something wrong so they walked over to George's house. Realising that the horse was covered with blood, they rushed into the house. The shirt of George was soaked with blood, and blood still oozed from the wound on his head. The men helped him to sit and examined the wound. It was a deep gash, and the amount of blood he appeared to have lost caused them some concern.

"What happened," asked his wife as she helped him to remove his shirt.

"I was attacked."

"Attacked?" asked one of the men in the room in surprise. "By who?"

"I couldn't see. It was dark."

"Dem niggahs."

"Yes. It's got to be those people," said his wife who had

been told about the afternoon's incident with Spike.

"What people?" asked one of the men.

"The slaves on the Silverman plantation," she answered.

"You sure about that, George?"

"I have no doubts," he felt anger welling up in him.

"Dem niggahs have to pay for this."

"You right. We goin' git 'em," one of them said and headed for the door.

As soon as George gave the men the indication that the attack could have been committed by the slaves on the plantation, the three men rushed out of the house. Within minutes, the pounding hoofs of horses approached the home of George Williams, the three riders carrying rifles. With the men screaming and vowing to kill the niggers, a few other people emerged from their homes to see what all the shouting and commotion was about. Soon after the men arrived, George also emerged with a white bandage around his head and climbed unto his horse. The four horsemen took off in the direction of the Silverman plantation. Realising that it would be useless to search the area of the attack for the attacker, the men rode on to their destination.

The noise of the approaching horses as usual, caused the dogs to start barking, and the barking announced the arrival of guests. This time the guests were unwelcome at the plantation, especially at that time of the evening. It was a moonlit night and the evening breeze was beautiful but, the events of the afternoon had most of the slaves worried and depressed. As a result, they all stayed in their shacks.

George and his horsemen rode directly to the slave quarters, dismounting about twenty yards from the shack of Spike and his roommate. Some of the slaves, who looked out to see who the guests were, watched the four white men approach the shack with rifles. They were led by the man with a blood-soaked bandaged head whom they later recognised as Devil George. It became evident to some of the slaves that George had been attacked and Spike was the suspect. Many of the slaves emerged from their rooms wondering what was going on. However, the sight of the men holding guns caused some of them to retreat into the safety of their rooms. Nevertheless, a few of them including Mae, Daisy Rae and Jackie together with some men walked cautiously toward Spike's room wondering why the white men were there. The whole situation did not make any sense to the slaves because John had not been seen leaving the quarters or running back into the room from anywhere. In fact, he had just returned to his room from Mae's place after a visit at the insistence of Spike to find out the likelihood of Mr. Silverman selling him. The slaves had all been concerned about Spike but the sight of the armed white men gave them a greater cause for concern.

"Niggahs, come out o' that rat hole," shouted one of the men.

"I'm going to count to three and burn the shack if you don't come out," threatened one of them.

"Spike," called George who felt that Spike could not have committed the crime but could be threatened to point out who did.

John emerged from the room holding a piece of cloth he appeared to be nursing the wounds of Spike with, followed by Spike who had no shirt on. The two slaves stood in front of their door wondering who or what the white men were looking for. Spike wondered why he had been picked on again. Nothing made sense to him, but staring at the barrel of the guns made him understand that he was only one shot

164

away from death. He looked very confused and frightened, and so did John. Meanwhile, Mae and her group had gotten closer to George and his men, and were standing about ten yards behind them. The sight of the two unarmed and innocent looking black men standing in front of the white men with guns, looked frightening because the slaves knew that attacking a white man meant the death sentence. And it was evident that George had been attacked. By whom, no one could tell. However, none of the slaves could understand why Spike and his roommate would be the suspects. It just did not make sense, and that was what all the slaves thought. But, no one had the courage or the power to challenge the white men.

"Boooy, did you attack George?" one of the men bellowed like an enraged buffalo.

"No massuh," answered Spike.

"Then who damn did?"

"I doan kno' massuh."

"Booy, you either tell me or you die," he said, pointing his gun.

"Ples, ples massuh I doan kno."

"I'll to count to three, Booy."

"Massuh I doan kno," he pleaded as he fell to his knees.

"You hear me, Booy?"

John was still standing, looking confused like a deer caught in a fog light.

"Massuh doan shoot me. I done no wron."

"I'm goin' to count, Boooy."

"Massuh, Suh, I doan kno," responded Spike who had started to perspire profusely.

John tried to speak but didn't quite know what to say. He took a quick look at Spike on the ground with a gun aimed at him and realised that they were both in serious danger. There was tension in the air as the two black men who had been convicted by being the most likely suspects stood hopelessly and helplessly before George and his men. All the slaves also looked on helplessly trying to make sense of the whole confrontation. George appeared not to be sure of what was going on because he was usually in command of situations and for someone else to be in control of a situation that directly affected him seemed unusual. His movements seemed tentative and he was not usually like that. Some of the slaves thought that the wound on his head may have probably affected his judgment and abilities.

Standing about two steps behind the inquisitor, George turned around and glanced at the slaves behind them with a look of uncertainty. It was obvious that he was thinking and wondering if he was at the right place. Picking on Spike was the logical thing to do, but it certainly did not look right at that point in time. The sight of the two slaves standing before them did not show guilt in any way. The picture clearly showed that Spike and John could not have attacked George, and George knew that. He also knew that no matter what the crime was, he could not just walk on to Mr. Silverman's plantation and execute his slaves without his permission. Nevertheless, he felt that their presence and the threat of execution would at least lead to the identification of the perpetrators of the attack.

One thing George was not sure of was how his friends were going to react to any decision inconsistent with their expectations. He realised that he was no longer in control of the situation, and with the count about to begin, the worst could happen. It was obvious that his colleagues were obsessed, in control of the situation and not thinking about the consequences of killing Mr. Silverman's slaves without his knowledge. He knew that the men were ready to shoot whoever was guilty and any words short of an order from him to let the slaves off the hook meant death to the slaves. That would certainly create problems for him and make him accountable to Mr. Silverman. Especially if it turned out that the wrong men were executed.

As soon as the lead inquisitor started the count, John summoned all the courage in his shaken body and directly appealed to George, "Massuh George, we no do nuffin."

"Two!" the count continued.

"So who threw the rock?" interrupted George as he moved to stand in front of the man doing the counting. He had regained control of the situation with his position.

"Massuh, we kno' nuffin, and the good Lawd kno' dat we no do nuffin."

"All right Booys, you are going to find me who attacked me."

"Yeb, massuh we gon tra," said John realising that there was nothing else they could say to change the situation.

"I'll give you to tomorrow morning," he threatened to the surprise of his friends.

"Yeb massuh," answered John.

"You hear, Booys?" he said to Spike.

"Yeb massuh."

"Yeb, suh," repeated John.

George then walked closely to Spike who was kneeling on the floor, bent down to him and whispered with clenched teeth, "I will kill you, if you don't tell me who did this to me."

"Yeb," Spike said feebly without even thinking about the implications.

"You hear?" yelled George.

"Yeb Massuh."

"Or I will tear your head off," pointing the gun to Spike's head.

"Yeb Massuh George."

"Tomorrow morning?"

"Massuh, I doan..." Spike tried to speak.

"You will tell me, Booy," George ordered.

"Yeb Massuh," answered Spike realising that, that was the only answer the white men wanted to hear.

When George turned around from the two slaves it became clear to the other white men that the execution had been called off. He made a quick jerk of his head to the colleague who still had his gun aimed at the slaves and the man lowered his gun. The man looked at George wondering why he was letting the slaves off for what they had done to him. As George walked past his friends, they turned and reluctantly followed him. Going past the slaves who had gathered, he spat out tobacco and climbed onto his horse. His colleagues also jumped on their horses and without saying another word, rode off into the night with all the slaves breathing a collective sigh of relief.

Spike remained on the floor crying, with John standing over him frozen in place. Mae, Jackie and Daisy Rae joined them with a few other slaves and tried to comfort them. Jackie also started to cry. They had all seen the first attempted execution of one of their family members and that had scared and shaken them to the core of their souls. Mae helped Spike off the floor and into his room with the rest of them following in silence. John remained outside still rooted to where he spoke his last life-saving words to George, wondering what might have been. Those in the room also wondered if they really came close to witnessing an execution. No one spoke for a few minutes as Spike and his sister continued to sob. Finally, John entered the room and said, "Tis gon be alrah. Tis gon be alrah, I premis."

In spite of his self-assured nature and composure, all the slaves in the room could see that John was much shaken. None of them had come that close to death. The perspiration on John's forehead was a clear indication of how scared he was. However, if he was that scared at the time of the confrontation, it did not show. In fact, his confidence and self-assured disposition during the confrontation may have also influenced the behaviour of George. Nevertheless, both Spike and John had made a promise to George and whether they were aware of the seriousness of the commitment they made was not evident. What mattered after the departure of George and his men was that their lives had been spared. At least for the time being.

When all the slaves retreated to their room after about an hour of analysis, and weighing of the gravity of the situation, Spike sat motionless on his bed while John sat rooted to the floor as they looked at each other. Spike did not know whether to ask if John had anything to do with the attack. He did not have any reason to think so because John had been with him all evening and could not have participated in any attack on George. He was, however, aware that the influence of John reached very far, even on the other plantations of Mr. Silverman but he could not determine when John could have planned an attack on George.

Sitting on the floor, John also had several thoughts running through his head at top speeds. He wondered what Spike was thinking about and felt strongly that Spike wanted to ask him if he had anything to do with the attack. Thus, trying to satisfy the curiosity of Spike, he moved over to sit next to him and put his arm around his shoulder. John whispered in the ear of Spike as if there were other people in the room eavesdropping. He pulled away from Spike and with a stern look on his face said, "Wha' d'you tink, Spike?"

"Huh?" said Spike with a look of surprise.

"I say wha' d'yew tink?"

"I doan kno' John."

"I mean.."

"Wha'?"

"Wha' we gon tell Debil George timoro?"

"I doan kno' John," he repeated and added, "Dem white fokes gwine kill us."

"Uh ah," John said shaking his head.

"Yeb."

"No, Spike. Debil George kno' we no attack him."

"Why yew say dat?"

"Becos dem white fokes will kill us. Debil George kno' yew no do it. He kno' dat I no go anywhar."

"So wha' he gon do?"

"He wan' us fine dem peple who do dat to 'im."

"How we gon do dat?"

"I tink tonat."

"I fear, John, I fear bad."

"Spike, leme tell ya sometin. Ebery man in dis worl' tink sometams. Eben Debil George tink. He tink. Dat's wha he come look for we. He tink dat he whup ya so we and some slabes attack 'im. Bot he kno' dat you no do nuffin. Yew no well. Yew hurt. Yew no stron'. How Debil George will kill yew? He kno' dat you no feel good to do nuffin to him. Yew no stron'. You weak. He kin tink dat some slaves attack him becos of wha' he do to yew. If so, he can kill ya. He's gon need ouah hep to catch dem peple. So he do nuffin to us. He's gon tra to harm we so we tell 'im wha he tink we kno', bot he's no gon kill we. Rah?

"I doan kno," responded Spike who did not know what to make of John's analysis.

"We gon be alrah Spike, we gon be alrah."

"Yeah?"

"Yeb."

"Yew kno' dat?

"Yeb."

"Alrah."

"Jes tink abou tit."

"I kint tink, John."

"Tra."

Spike always believed in John, but this time his confidence was shaken. Nevertheless, he still could trust his judgment. John has always been the trusted friend he has known since they arrived together on the plantation over ten years ago. As a result, he had no reason to believe that John would lead him to death because guns had been pointed at them that evening. Even in the face of death, Spike believed in the wisdom of his friend.

Lying in his bed a couple of hours after the confrontation, Spike wondered if the darkness was indeed the cover that the white men needed to sneak up on them and kill them. The faces of the white men seemed to appear in the dark, mocking and threatening him with death. He managed to convince himself that the faces were of his own imagination. But then, he still felt that the door of the room could come crashing down any moment, followed by real white faces. He had become sensitive to every sound in the neighbourhood. The sounds of the crickets and other insects seemed louder than ever but he did not really care about the noises of the insects. He was only concerned about the sounds of feet or horses that could be approaching the slave quarters. He tried to discern noises, which did not even exist to determine which ones were friendly and innocent or a threat to his life. Sweat poured over his body profusely and the joy of sleep seemed several thousand years away as he tossed and turned, worried and endured the pain from his wounds. Meanwhile, John snored soundly in peaceful sleep.

Spike's mind wandered until the wee hours of the morning and could wander no more. The mind was drained and his body was weak. He could not fight sleep anymore. The likelihood that he would have the chance to resist his pursuers was slipping away as sleep tried to sneak up on him. Slowly, and unknowingly, he was consumed by the power of sleep and his mind slipped into the realm of dreams.

CHAPTER 9

*I*t's been two days since the attack on George. The days following the attack had been the most difficult for all the slaves at the hands of George. As a result of his wounds from the beating, Spike had also not been able to work on the farm for two days. But with the help of his sister, he healed quickly. George seemed not to care about the absence of Spike and he did not make an issue of it as he would ordinarily have done. He appeared to have accepted the fact that Spike could not have attacked him or participated in the attack. However, he had a strong conviction that some of the slaves who sympathised with Spike may have attacked him, and for that Spike had to be held accountable. In all his thoughts and focus on a single person, George had forgotten that there were scores of other slaves who hated him with every breath they took. He had even forgotten that there was also a Silverman in the mansion of the plantation who wasn't very fond of him. Nevertheless, he did not care much about Catherine Silverman's feelings toward him, because her father wielded the ultimate power and that was all he cared about. Besides, he was not fond of Catherine either and was confident that she could not hurt him in any way.

It was unusual for George to go the Silverman mansion in the morning before going to work on the plantation.

However, this morning was an unusual morning, because Mr. Silverman was upset at the report he received from Mae regarding the attempted murder of his slaves. When George was ushered into the house by one of the servants, he felt the tension in the air because the always, polite Mr. Silverman was not at the door to meet him as he always did. A house servant pointed George to the door leading to the study and left. George entered the study followed by Catherine who emerged from the kitchen, with her mother also trailing as they all entered the study. Mr. Silverman had his head buried in a book when George walked in. Turning around to see George, he let out a muted gasp at the sight of his heavily bandaged head. It appeared George had added on extra layers of bandage to exaggerate his condition, and by the look on Mr. Silverman's face, it seemed to work.

Mr. Silverman had been upset all morning about what he heard from Mae and had prepared to show his displeasure in the harshest way to George. That was going to be the first time Mr. Silverman had either yelled at him or talked down to him. However, the sight of George completely changed his mood and thoughts. He felt sorry for the pain George could be going through and that clearly showed on his face. Catherine on the other hand was very opinionated, detail-oriented and made her opinion known to George that he was wrong for even attempting to murder his father's slaves on their own property. To make sure that she would not miss George that morning and have the opportunity to tell him what was on her mind, Catherine stayed close to her father until George arrived.

With his anger somewhat dissolved in uncertain sympathy, Mr. Silverman calmly asked George to sit down. George still felt that his boss was upset despite the calmness he exhibited.

"Are you all right?" asked Mr. Silverman of his plantation manager.

"I've seen better mornings, Mr. Silverman."

"Are you sure?"

"Yes sir."

"Is it a big wound?"

"It's a very deep cut."

"Well what happened?" asked Mr. Silverman.

"Mmm, mmm," Catherine cleared her throat realising that they were about to listen to a sugar-coated version of the story.

George gave a detailed account of his ordeal and his attempt to find the people who attacked him with his friends. Even though he did not stress on the confrontation with the slaves, thus, creating the impression that he had gone to the slave quarters to solicit the help of Spike and his roommate to find the perpetrators, the story Mr. Silverman had heard from Mae and the other servants was very different. Yet still Mr. Silverman did not exhibit any anger. He rationalised that George must have been extremely angry and that may have clouded his judgment. After all, no harm was done to his slaves, he thought. Catherine, on the hand, did not share the sentiments of her father and felt that George should be made aware of his mistake lest he repeated it in the future.

Showing no sympathy for the man whom his father had treated gently, Catherine moved closer to her father to give the impression that she was speaking for him.

"You should know better George, than to bring people on to my father's property to kill his slaves without his permission," Catherine said, looking straight into the eyes of George.

"I did not come here to kill any slaves."

"You didn't. And what about the other men?"

"They could not have done anything to the slaves without my permission."

"Whose permission?" Catherine asked sharply.

"I meant…" George tried to speak.

"Your permission?"

"No."

"I hope not."

"Catherine, George says he only came to threaten and I don't doubt him," said Mr. Silverman.

"But I do."

"Well let's leave it at that."

"Why, Father?"

"Because nothing happened to the slaves."

"But he came here to do harm."

"He says he didn't and I don't doubt him."

"Well, I do."

"Catherine," her mother called.

She turned around, looked at her mother and quickly left the room.

Mister Silverman watched his daughter leave without saying a word. He realised that saying anything else could prolong the conversation, and that made George uncomfortable. He looked at his wife and threw his arms in the air as Catherine closed the door.

"George, I hope your wound heals quickly."

"Thank you, Sir."

"I'll help find whoever attacked you if the person is indeed on this plantation."

"Yes Sir."

"Well."

"I am very sorry for what happened here last night," George said.

"You have to be very careful," Mrs. Silverman cautioned.

"Yes, Maam."

"All right. Take care of the wound."

"Yes Sir," he responded and stood up to leave.

George was aware that Mr. Silverman meant well but there was nothing he could do to find those who attacked him. The best he could do was sympathise with him and give him all the support he could to find the perpetrators of the attack. George also knew that he had to find the men himself and he was determined to do just that, even if it meant offending Catherine Silverman in the process.

Subsequently, the tension on the farm became unbearable for the slaves as George and his slave-driving colleagues overworked the slaves and used all kinds of torturous means to try and find his attackers. Hoping that the female slaves would break under his constant pressure, he repeatedly threatened and overworked them and made sure that all the slaves worked extra long hours. After two weeks of this tactic and constant interrogation of the slaves without any leads to his attackers, it became clear to George that his attackers would never be found.

The slaves had withstood his assault, and the harvesting season was coming to an end rather quickly. He was however satisfied with the work done by the slaves because not only was harvesting completed in record time, but he also had an opportunity to make more money. In the long run, George rationalised that if he could not find his attackers, he was going to earn more money for the work done by the slaves. He appeared to welcome the monetary reward than the endless pursuit of the slaves who attacked him. He had accepted defeat at the hands of the slaves and much as he hated it, there was nothing he could do about it. The worst treatment of the slaves had not yielded one of the desired results for George.

Exactly fifteen days after the attack on George, the harvesting at the cotton plantation was completed and the pressure on the slaves seemed to ease. To the slaves, the world seemed to be a better place once again. How long their feelings would last did not really matter to them. The days that lay ahead in the future did not hold any promises of freedom, and they were aware of that. However, they were alert enough to realise that their experiences of happiness were usually short-lived and it was an unpardonable sin not to take advantage of the opportunities that presented themselves. The experiences of tomorrow might not be the same, and time has thought them well.

There was happiness in the air. Catherine's wedding was a week away. It was time to relax and enjoy the short break the moment presented.

*   *   *

Two days before the wedding, the Silverman mansion was full of activity in preparation for the wedding. The grounds were beautifully groomed with every shrub, flower and grass in perfect shape, and all rocks in their right places. Catherine's twin cousins, Mary and Magdalene Wilson had arrived from Charleston with their parents and the house was unusually noisy. Unmarried and in their early twenties, the Wilson girls were very attractive, spoiled and eager to meet men at the wedding. All the time they spent helping Catherine and her parents to prepare for the wedding was spent talking about and assessing the men who will be coming to the wedding. They spent time gossiping, trying on clothes with their cousins, practicing how to dance with Catherine's only sibling, Jack Jr. who had also arrived from Harvard Law School in Massachusetts for the wedding.

The festive atmosphere in the Silverman mansion spilled over into the slave quarters where the slaves also enjoyed the perceived break from hard work. The relaxed atmosphere prevailed through the wedding day. Even though the slaves were not allowed very close to the wedding ceremony, most of them dressed up in beautiful clothing and stayed at a distance to witness the marriage of the favourite daughter on the plantation. The dancing and partying after the ceremony continued late into the night in the grand hall of the Silverman mansion until the last guest left at about eight o'clock in the evening. The Wilson twins had managed to pair themselves with two handsome friends of Jack Jr., who had accompanied him home from Massachusetts. With the parents of the Wilson sisters and the Silvermans seeming to approve of the partnerships that had developed during the wedding, a mini party continued in the house after all the guests had left.

Meanwhile activities had also picked up considerably at the slave quarters and the "Tree Bottom" was alive with music. Jackie and the other slaves sang several beautiful songs as they danced and Mae and Uncle Josef told short and funny stories. As the night progressed, the singing took on a new character as the clapping, feet stomping and merry making appeared to seep into the Silverman mansion. The singing at the slave quarters grew louder and sweeter and that attracted the occupants of the Silverman mansion who started to look at each other and wondered if it was not time to find out what all the merry making at the slave quarters was all about. The Wilson sisters and their male companions were more interested than the others because the songs sounded so good and the whole celebration was a new experience for them.

At the urging of Jack Jr., the Silverman's and their remaining guests in the mansion walked over to the "Tree Bottom" to enjoy the songs of the slaves. Their smiling and happy faces were illuminated by the large fire in the middle of the celebration. After listening to one song, the Wilson sisters and their friends jumped into the circle of celebration and started stomping their feet and dancing with some of the slaves. Catherine and Anthony also joined the dancing and soon there was another party of masters and slaves going on; but this time on the turf of the slaves. With the parents of the Silverman and Wilson girls looking on from the porch, the celebration went on for a few minutes before the masters retreated to their mansion with smiles in exhaustion. To Catherine, the dancing at 'Tree Bottom' was a fitting end to a beautiful wedding because she had a special connection with Jackie and Mae, and being among them for that short moment made her very happy. She had kept her promise to Jackie that she would dance with her at "Tree Bottom".

*   *   *

The Silvermans asked Anthony and his wife to make their home in their huge mansion after their marriage because there was more than enough room for three families. Besides, the Smiths did not have a house big enough for the new couple and their new housemaid, Jackie. The seed that Catherine planted in her father's head long before the wedding bore fruit in the form of a piano. One of Mr. and Mrs. Silverman's presents to the newlyweds was a piano. Anthony could not thank the Silvermans enough because he had no means to purchase a piano and his father would not part with the piano in their home, especially since there were younger Smiths in the house. The Smiths were all good musicians and always had a piano in their home. Thus, living without a piano and beautiful music was an experience Catherine was not sure her husband could deal with. Anthony started playing the piano before he turned five, and he played almost every day of his life.

On the evening that he knelt down like a proper Southern gentleman to propose to Catherine, he also promised to teach her to play the piano. Soon after their wedding, Anthony started to teach his wife to play the piano. Being home, Catherine practiced constantly with the aim of surprising her father at how good she had gotten on the instrument. She was motivated to impress her father. When she was not busy, Jackie sat next to Catherine as she practiced on the piano and would sometimes teach Jackie words to songs so she could sing along. Catherine loved to hear Jackie sing so she encouraged her to sing or hum to tunes, especially hymns she had managed to teach her. Catherine's face always glowed whenever Jackie sang and hit the highest notes of songs that revealed her rich and powerful voice. The two women enjoyed their times together.

One late afternoon, Anthony came home unexpectedly from his hardware store and saw the two women engrossed in their music. The women did not hear Anthony enter the room. He listened to them until they finished, and startled them when he applauded. He congratulated his wife, kissed her and patted Jackie on the shoulder. Jackie shot a strained smile at him and quickly left the room, saying, "Massuh Anteny wan res".

"All right, Jackie you may go now," responded Catherine.

Since moving into the Silverman mansion three months ago, Anthony had not made any physical contact with Jackie until that afternoon when he patted her on the shoulder. In fact, it was his first physical contact with her in over ten years. Catherine did not see the strained smile on Jackie's face otherwise, she would have realised that the smile was awkward and not typical of the sweet seductive smile that illuminated her face on occasions like that. Upon entering the kitchen, Jackie began to brush her shoulder vigorously as she muttered to herself. She felt the handprints of Anthony on her shoulder from the patting and she could not bear the thought of that. Catherine heard the sounds from the kitchen as Jackie vigorously brushed her shoulder, but she was accompanying her husband up the stairs so she ignored the strange sounds. She suspected, however, that Jackie was unhappy about something but could not tell what, especially since the sounds seemed to contradict the happy atmosphere that just preceded it. She looked at her husband quizzically but he paid no attention as they climbed the stairs.

*   *   *

It has been eleven years since Jack Silverman bought a dozen slaves from a rich farmer who sold his entire farm together with his slaves and moved west. That was how Mae and her entire family including Jackie and her brother ended up at the Silverman plantation. As a result of her previous experience, Mae was recommended to work in the kitchen. Catherine was a young girl then going to school with her big brother John Jr., who was also her best friend and someone she looked up to. Thus, a major void was created in her life when a few years after the arrival of the new slaves her brother left to go to law school in Boston. Soon after her brother's departure, Catherine became lonely, unhappy and felt like an only child. However, over a period of time, she developed a strong attachment to Jackie and eased the concerns of her parents. Jackie was a few years older than Catherine, very pleasant and liked by the Silvermans so they encouraged her friendship with their daughter. As they became closer, Jackie was asked to attend to the needs of Catherine in addition to her other chores in the Silverman house. It was an honour for the slave because it brought her closer to the master's favourite person and gave her access to one of the influential persons on the plantation. All the slaves had become aware that Catherine was the apple of her father's eye and was the only one who could get through to Mr. Silverman even when her mother was having difficulties penetrating the complex-natured man.

After being together for ten years, it also did not surprise anyone when Jackie became the housemaid of Anthony and Catherine after their marriage. Catherine had gotten very close to Jackie and could not imagine functioning effectively without the services of Jackie. Anthony, on the other hand could live without the discomfort of seeing Jackie every day. Anthony's discomfort caused him to speak erratically and sometimes irrationally when he was in the company of Jackie. Catherine had seen that uncomfortable behaviour in Anthony but she paid it no particular attention.

About six months after Jackie's arrival at the Silverman plantation, Senator Smith's wife left him. The constant fights between the couple resulting from the senator's affair with a female slave had progressively become embarrassing; the topic of gossips among friends was so unpleasant that she moved out of the house, leaving the senator and their three children. Prior to her departure and at the height of their fights, Missus Smith banned all slaves from the house and got rid of the lone female slave who worked in the house. Thus, with no help and conditions in the house getting worse, the Silvermans felt obligated to do whatever they could to resolve the situation. All their efforts to keep the marriage of their friends together failed when Missus Smith left.

The Smith household needed help and someone to cook and maintain the house until a permanent maid was found. At the suggestion of Mrs. Silverman, Jackie's services were volunteered to the Smiths. Jackie knew enough about housekeeping and cooking from working with Mae to be helpful to the Smiths. In Missus Silverman's opinion she could hold the house together for the few weeks it would take to find and train a new housemaid.

From the time Jackie entered the Smiths house, she never felt comfortable. She especially did not like the stares of Anthony Smith who at nineteen was the eldest of the Smith children and eleven years older than the next child. Obviously, the Smiths had never seen such a beautiful slave before. Missus Smith would definitely have driven her and out off her grounds even before she set foot in the house. Senator Smith was still reeling from the scandal and the departure of his wife to appreciate the beauty of Jackie. Anthony on the other hand had his hormones overflowing and could not help himself with fantasies about Jackie. Despite the problems of his parents, he rationalised that there had to be something special about the slaves that was the reason his father slept with them. In his case, he was not married and so could fantasise about the most beautiful slave, if not woman, he had ever seen.

Under adverse and uncomfortable conditions, Jackie managed to adjust to her new environment and was approaching the end of her second week in the Smith household. On one rainy evening, Jackie was alone in the kitchen preparing the evening meal. The house was quite except for the raindrops that beat hard on the window and the wild frightening booms of the thunderstorm. The children were upstairs and the senator was not expected until late in the evening. The unceasing loud thunderstorms were later interrupted with a more beautiful sound of the piano as Anthony started to play. The first time Jackie heard the piano was in the Smith's house and she was fascinated with the instrument. She was not allowed near the instrument so she could not get close enough to examine this amazing machine. As soon as Anthony started to play the piano, Jackie took a peek at him as she always did through the kitchen door, trying to understand how the instrument worked. After a brief moment of listening, she went back to cooking. Shortly after, the piano music stopped. She kept thinking and wondering how that big box of a machine produced those sounds while admiring the talents of Anthony.

Suddenly and unexpectedly, she felt a moist hand on her neck. Immediately she knew whose hand that was. She froze for a moment as she wondered what was going on as the white hands appeared to turn her around. She stiffened her body and tried to push Anthony away, but she realised that her strength was not enough as he tightened his grip on her. With one swift move, he forced Jackie down to the floor. A struggle ensued as Anthony moved up her dress but Jackie could still not ward of her stronger attacker. Her cries were not and could not be heard as the rain began to come down harder. Anthony thrust himself on the slave and started to rape her. Jackie's screams did not stop him as he continued with the attack.

Afterwards, Jackie lay on the kitchen floor as excruciating pain shot through her body. She let out a hard scream and like a wounded tiger, got up from the floor and flew through the kitchen door into the thunderstorm crying and with cold rain beating on her face. She began to run in the dark and ran all the way on instinct to the Silverman plantation about two miles away.

Mae and Daisy Rae were chatting when suddenly Jackie burst into the room, soaking wet. Mae and her sister were dumbfounded and shocked at the sight of Jackie who held on to Mae, breathing heavily and trying to speak. Mae collected herself and with a worried look inquired, "Wha' happun Jackie, Wha' happun?"

Daisy Rae looked out to see if there was someone following Jackie but did not see anyone in the dark. She quickly turned around to see Jackie collapse in the arms of Mae before they could ask any more questions. They frantically changed her wet clothes, covered her with a blanket and started to wipe her down with warm water. Shortly after, Jackie opened her eyes but did not say a word as the women inquired about what had happened and why she had ran home from the Smiths. Mae could only guess from her torn dress that she had either been attacked or driven out of the house. But she could not understand why the Smiths would drive her out of the house, especially since she was there to help, and Jackie was not the type to hurt anyone let alone the children. She left Jackie alone for a moment, but Daisy Rae was impatient and worried, so she shot questions at Jackie, demanding to know what had happened.

"Who hurt yew?"

"Daisy Rae," Mae tried to interrupt.

"Baby, I say wha' happun to yew?"

"Daisy Rae, lef har, she kin' talk naw."

"Somebode hur' dat chal' Mae."

"I kno' dat."

"And am gwine fan out."

"Les wait to timoro come."

"Ma God, wha' dis?"

They refused to speculate aloud as to what could have happened, knowing that Senator Smith had had an affair with a slave before. However, Mae did not think that the elder Smith would and could do that to Jackie especially since he had just lost his wife for fooling around with a slave and was having a bad time dealing with the consequences. Their minds kept wandering, imagining and wondering what could have happened as Jackie lay there looking at them without saying a word.

A few days after the incident, Catherine asked Jackie why she had suddenly come back from the Smiths and she told her and Mrs. Silverman that she developed a high fever and only Mae could treat her that's why she came back home. Jackie did not tell anyone what actually happened even though Mae and her sister suspected that she had been sexually attacked or an attempt was made on her. The effect of her experience changed her attitude and demeanour during the days that followed. Catherine realised the change in Jackie and complained to her mother, but Missus Silverman assured her that the sickness may have caused her to behave that way and for Catherine to give her time to recover. Realising that her demeanour was beginning to attract attention and questions, Jackie snapped out of her moods. She did not want the issue to be brought up again or anyone to suspect that she had been raped so she made serious efforts to become her old bubbly, ever smiling and sweet self. The change in her mood and attitude confirmed Missus Silverman's explanation to her daughter. Without consulting Jackie, Mae managed to convince Mrs. Silverman not to send Jackie back to the Smith's house. Jackie had also sworn to herself never to go back to that house again under any circumstance and was prepared for whatever lay ahead if she defied Missus Silverman. Luckily, Mr. Smith found a new housemaid shortly after Jackie's departure.

A few weeks after the incident, it became evident to Mae and Daisy Rae that Jackie was pregnant, thus confirming their suspicions. The women panicked at the thought of explaining how Jackie had gotten pregnant. Once again they tried to find out what actually happened when the signs of pregnancy began to manifest themselves, but Jackie did not tell them anything except that she was attacked on her way home. The explanation did not make any sense to Mae and Daisy Rae but rather than push, they decided to give it time.

The women continued to worry because they could not imagine the enormity of the scandal that was about to explode into the open. How were they or Jackie going to explain the pregnancy of a woman who was not married? Who was the father? All the slaves knew that it was an abomination and in fact, unheard of for any woman in their community to sleep with a man to whom she was not married. Besides, it was a small slave community, and if Jackie was sleeping with anyone, all the slaves would know. As a result, Mae and Daisy Rae could not begin to even think about all the questions that will be asked, let alone the answers. Meanwhile, Jackie's moods began to swing again to the other extreme when she realised that she was pregnant. There was pressure on Mae to limit Jackie's exposure to Missus Silverman until she found some answers or until the problem came out in the open naturally. The pressures of the days made the days seem like weeks. Jackie was also becoming cagey and unfriendly and some of the slaves had begun noticing the change in her attitude, but none of them suspected that she was pregnant. Life had become rather difficult for the three women involved and it did not look like it was going to be any easier in the coming weeks.

Laying in her bed and wondering how she was going to sleep through another night of worries, questions with no answers and the weight of the world on her shoulders, Mae heard a muted cry from Jackie. Daisy Rae also heard the sound and quickly turned around to see what was happening to the pregnant woman. Mae got up, picked up a lantern and with Daisy Rae following, approached Jackie. They stared emptily at each other wondering what was going on with Jackie. As soon as Mae started to ask Jackie what was wrong with her, they noticed the bed was soaked with blood. Mae suddenly collected herself and got a pail of water standing in the corner of the room. She motioned Daisy Rae to get a towel, and together they began to clean the shocked and crying woman who was bleeding with lots of clots. Working in silence amidst the sobs of Jackie, the two women cleaned her up and disposed of all the bloody clothing under the cover of darkness.

When morning came, Mae and Daisy Rae went about their routine with mixed feelings, but did not show any emotion or signs of the traumatic experience of the previous night. Mae had made an excuse for the slave masters on

Jackie's behalf, so she told Jackie to stay in bed for the day. Luckily, no one bothered to visit her and Mae did not make any special effort to prevent her brother from visiting her when he learned that his sister was not well. Mae knew that Spike was not sophisticated enough to detect that Jackie was pregnant or there was anything amiss. At the end of the day when the three women got together in their shack, very little was said except the usual words to find out how Jackie was doing. When everything seemed to be all right with her, they all broke down in tears, holding on to each other in the middle of the room and thanking Jesus.

Was it tears of relief because the scandal would not cascade into serious problems for them, or was it for the miscarriage and the loss of a baby? There were still many questions to be asked but none of them knew where to begin, and more importantly, they were not sure whether they wanted to know the answers or where the questions would lead. For Jackie, there was relief. For the other two women, there was hurt and more questions wrapped in sheaths of relief. The sense of relief and the trust they had for each other seemed to be the only bond that kept them together. They had also developed a strong mistrust for people and as the days rolled into weeks, the weeks into months and the months into years, the bonds between them grew stronger.

*   *   *

When Catherine came down, breakfast was ready. She had asked Jackie not to bother with breakfast for them because she could take care of that. Jackie, on the other hand did not think that making breakfast was any work. Besides, it was a good opportunity for her to listen to the usual Anthony's morning piano music. Mr. Smith had made it a habit of playing the piano every morning because it pleased his wife immensely, but Jackie also enjoyed it from the confines of the kitchen as she prepared breakfast.

On this beautiful morning, Anthony followed his wife to the kitchen to compliment Jackie for the wonderful cinnamon bread she had baked for breakfast. Anthony had watched the friendship between his wife and Jackie develop into a strong bond of trust over the years and wanted to be part of it. He had tried in his mind to share in the friendship but he could not. He had also realised since his rape of Jackie over ten years ago, how stupid, barbaric and inconsiderate he had been, and was looking for an opportunity to apologise. However, he did not know how and felt ashamed and impotent to bring up the subject with Jackie. Not being able to apologise or do anything about the barrier that had been erected between him and Jackie, he resorted to complete avoidance of his victim. Anthony felt strongly that no one knew of the attack otherwise the Silvermans would have heard about it, especially since Mae and Daisy Rae were that close to Catherine's parents. Additionally, there was no doubt in his mind that Catherine would not have married him if she had any knowledge of the rape or even an attempted rape. It had been a mental torture for him for many years and especially now, since he wanted to be a part of the friendship the women had. Catherine wanted that more than anything else, because she sensed that there was something missing between the three of them as a unit and she felt that was the only blemish on her marriage. In spite of her wishes, she did not pressure Anthony to get closer to Jackie. She believed that it was only a matter of time when they will all develop the friendship and trust she wished for.

"After all they lived in the same house and whatever discomforts Anthony had with a female slave as a result of his father's experience could be healed with time and Jackie's charm," Catherine thought.

Anthony came home from work earlier than his wife anticipated. After spending some time in the living room, they retreated upstairs.

"Catherine darling?" he seemed to question as he stretched his body on the bed with his eyes focused on the ceiling.

"Yes Anthony."

"I need to talk to you about Jackie."

"I was hoping you would."

"Why do you say that?"

"I think there's something missing."

"What do you mean?"

"Well."

"Can you explain that," Anthony cut in.

"Yes. You know I love Jackie. She is one of the closest people in my life and I would want you to be close to her. I can't expect you to love her as much as I do."

"Well."

"Well, what? I think it will bring us all together."

"I know that Catherine."

"Then why do you maintain this distance with her?"

"What distance?" he probed.

"I don't think you like her very much."

"On the contrary, I do."

"You do?"

"Yes I do."

"Hmmm. That's strange. Then, why the distance?" Jackie asked.

"I…"

"Well let me guess," interrupted Catherine.

"Go ahead."

"Does it have to do with your parents?"

Anthony did not answer. He really didn't know what to say. He was filled with emotion and had begun to wonder where the conversation would end and what it would reveal.

"Does it?" asked Catherine again.

"In a way, yes," he lied.

"Do you want to talk about it?"

"Not really, darling."

"But what has that got to do with Jackie?"

"Please let's leave it here for now."

"Why?"

"Because I've resolved it in my mind."

"Resolved what?"

"All the inhibitions I have about female slaves," he lied again and continued, "I will warm up to her and apologise for any fears and discomforts I have caused her."

"You don't have to apologise. Just warm up to her."

"No it's proper to apologise to her, because I have not made her comfortable," he insisted.

"All right, if that's what you want to do."

"Yes darling, I want to do that."

"Thank you, Anthony," said Catherine as she planted a kiss on his lip.

"I should thank you for bearing with me."

"I love you, Anthony."

"I love you too."

They started petting and not soon after it started, they laid there facing each other after making love.

"Anthony."

"Yes, Catherine," he whispered a response.

"Anthony?"

"Yes, darling?"

"That's better," she smiled.

"Catherine, I wanted…"

"Don't say anything," she interrupted.

"Okay," he said softly.

"I am going over to see Mama."

"Now?"

"Yes, so you can relax before dinner."

"Don't go yet," he said as he held on close to his wife for comfort and with some sort of relief that he had found some courage to approach Jackie and apologise.

"I'll be back sooner than you think, darling."

"You promise?"

"Don't be silly."

"All right."

"Jackie is preparing dinner, so I won't be long."

"Don't be long," he said and planted a kiss on his wife.

Jackie got up from bed, changed her clothes and left.

Anthony stayed in bed, his eyes focused on the ceiling and daydreaming. His mind finally settled on the events that occurred about a decade earlier. He wondered how life could have been better for everyone if he had not attacked that attractive young slave who had been brought over to help his family. He covered his face with a pillow and stayed motionless. He was filled with remorse and pain for what he now realised was a wonderful life he was missing. He had finally realised that the macho and stubborn front he had been wearing for the decade was indeed very weak and brittle. The time had come for him to try to remedy a situation that, in fact, was untenable. He stayed in bed for a while longer before dragging himself from bed and heading downstairs.

He felt a bit relieved and was confident that there was going to be an end to this dark blotch on his life that seemed to grow like cancer with each passing day.

Walking down the stairs, Anthony's eyes settled on the one object that gave him the peace he could not find in any other thing or person including his wife. He walked calmly to the piano and settled comfortably on the chair. He rolled around his head, stretched his arms and fingers like a concert pianist and started to play. He played two beautiful classical pieces and suddenly stopped at the beginning of a third song.

It suddenly occurred to him that there was something more important to do before his wife arrived. Anthony summoned all the courage he could, and headed for the kitchen. Just before he touched the kitchen door to open it, he froze not knowing whether to proceed, unsure of what response he would receive. He looked around to see if there was anyone watching, knowing very well that no one else could be in the house. Anthony was nervous. He looked at the ceiling, shook his head and wondered why he was making a big deal of the situation. He slowly opened the swing door without making any sound. When the door fully opened, he saw Jackie's backed turned as she peeled potatoes.

All of a sudden, Jackie felt a heavy presence in the room. She knew that the only person who could be in the kitchen was Anthony. Her heart started thumping as her experience of ten years ago kept flashing back. Her heart began to thump heavily. She felt strongly that Anthony would be making contact with her at any moment. Her hands began to tremble and the potato she was peeling dropped into the sink. At that point she swore in her heart that his soul would belong to the Almighty and his heart will belong to her if he attempted to rape. Anthony made a slow advance toward Jackie and softly called her name. She felt the cold hands of Mr. Smith on her shoulder. She had a flashback of the rape experience some ten years ago. And before he could say a word, Jackie swung the knife with a deadly force, stabbing him in the chest. Simultaneously, Anthony began to apologise and fell to the floor.

Jackie stayed on top of the wounded man muttering some strange words. She seemed possessed with rage. She removed the knife and stabbed the wooden floor two more times still screaming those strange words as Anthony apologised. He seemed to have frozen and become impotent as Jackie attacked. Just as violently as it had started, Jackie violently burst through the back door of the house and started running toward the Silverman plantation to the slave quarters. Her dress was soaked with blood and mud as she ran in the rain with the knife still in her hand. On the way, she fell three times from panic and exhaustion. On the third fall, she tripped and landed in a pool of muddy water and began wailing and screaming at the top of her voice asking, "What have I done, what have I done?" in Fante. She threw the knife into the pool, which appeared dark red and looked like blood to her. She stood up and started running hard toward the slave quarters, which was then in sight. With a few of the slaves watching her and wondering what was going on Jackie forcefully knocked down the door of the room she shared with Mae, Daisy Rae and the children and fell head first to the floor. She was knocked out cold.

CHAPTER 10

*T*he drums were still pounding heavily and Jackie's head was thumping and throbbing to the beat of the biggest and loudest drum. She could hear voices and the music getting closer but the heavy drum was so dominating that she could not distinguish between the voices or make any sense of what was being said. She, however, felt that she was getting closer to the source of the music and the voices with every step. Suddenly she seemed to hear the voice of her daughter calling. She started to run toward the music convinced that she would meet her family. When some cold liquid was thrown on her face, she woke up with the heavy drum still thumping, but this time she could hear the whole music with a beautiful melody.

Jackie stared into the face of the priestess who was standing over her and chanting. She continued her stare wondering where she was and why she was so wet and sitting on the floor in the dirt. Another priestess appeared and helped her up from the floor. She spoke in English to Jackie and covered her with a dry white cloth.

"What's going on?"

No one answered.

"Where am I, and where is my daughter?"

"You will be all right," was the answer of the priestess.

"Please, where is my daughter?"

"Follow me."

Jackie dragged her drained body behind the priestess and as they emerged from the back of the shrine, she seemed to remember the incidents of the evening before she became possessed. She stopped and asked the priestess again, "What happened?"

"You were possessed by Nana Benya."

"The god?"

"Yes."

"I have had the most terrifying dream," Jackie whispered.

"I'm sure," said the priestess not bothering to find out what the dream was about.

"Where are my daughter and friends?"

"Come with me."

The priestess led her from the back of the shrine, and as they emerged, some of the spectators began to cheer and clap their hands. As soon as Mae saw the two women emerge, she dragged the children to the edge of the shrine where the woman who had been possessed earlier on had exited. Together with Franco, they met and embraced Jackie. Ama and Bianca were crying not knowing what had been done to Jackie. She had been gone for about fifteen minutes.

"Maa you are wet."

"Yes, my baby, but I am all right. What happened?"

"Let's get out of here," pleaded Mae without answering Jackie's question.

"Take me home, please take me home I am cold."

"Maa, let's go."

With the help of Mae who wrapped her arm around Jackie, and with Franco holding the hands of the children, they moved away from the crowd and headed for their car as the drumming faded behind them several hundred yards away.

It was ten o'clock in the evening and to most of the people at the ceremony, Monday night was only beginning. To Jackie, the night had ended. However, there was a whole day of celebration at the Bakatue Festival the following afternoon, and for that she could not wait. She still had enough energy to fantasise about the tens of thousands of visitors and tourists that had descended onto Elmina to have fun and enjoy the festival.

"We will be back tomorrow," she said not sure whether it was a question or a statement.

"Yes we will," assured Mae.

Printed in the United States
By Bookmasters